Dalton and the Sundown Kid

When Dalton rides into Lonetree looking for work, he arrives in a town crippled by the local outlaw: the Sundown Kid. The Kid has a tight hold over the town, but Dalton's desperation for employment means he lands the task of resolving the newest kidnap situation. He is asked to deliver a ransom to the bandit in order to secure the safe return of the young Sera Culver.

Before Dalton reaches the rendezvous point however, disaster strikes and the ransom is stolen. A fearsome shootout leaves him stranded in the wilderness: no ransom, no girl, no bounty. With the fate of a young woman at stake, the ransom money to hunt down, and the Sundown Kid to bring to justice, can Dalton fight the good fight and help Lonetree prevail?

Dalton and the Sundown Kid

Ed Law

A Black Horse Western

ROBERT HALE · LONDON

© Ed Law 2014
First published in Great Britain 2014

ISBN 978-0-7198-1170-8

Robert Hale Limited
Clerkenwell House
Clerkenwell Green
London EC1R 0HT

www.halebooks.com

Typeset by
Derek Doyle & Associates, Shaw Heath
Printed and bound in Great Britain by
CPI Antony Rowe, Chippenham and Eastbourne

CHAPTER 1

Beyond the rise, a tendril of smoke was spiralling up into the sky.

Dalton reckoned the town of Lonetree was still an hour downriver and so he rubbed his right leg as he prepared to move quickly. The action eased the tension in a leg he'd broken last month.

The limb was splinted, which created its own problems by forcing him to ride stiffly. When he'd massaged the muscles back into life, he rode at a brisk trot and, after cresting the rise, his worst fears materialized.

Midway between the summit of the rise and Black Creek, a covered wagon lay on its side. Scuff marks on the ground suggested it had rolled too quickly down the slope and toppled, although the smouldering canvas hinted at a more sinister reason for its demise.

The only movement nearby came from a horse

mooching upriver, but as he saw nothing to concern him, he rode openly down the rise and then dismounted.

He stood on his good leg and rocked his splinted leg back and forth, easing the stiffness before he moved on. Although using a hobbling gait was quicker, he usually forced himself to walk as normally as he could and so it took him a minute to walk around the scene.

When he peered inside, nobody was there. The smoke had almost died out suggesting his first impression may have been wrong and this had been an accident after all.

He stood back with an idea taking shape that, after he'd spun the wheels and confirmed they were intact, fully grabbed his attention.

Aside from a broken bow, the wagon was usable, even if he was unsure how he could use it. But he reckoned a man who was looking for work but who had limited mobility might improve his chances if he had a small wagon.

He doubted that on his own he'd normally be able to right it, but the slope gave him a course of action and so he stood at the back and experimentally shoved the base. As it had come to rest in a precarious position, using only one hand he was able to gently rock the wagon.

He put his other hand to the task. He rocked it more strongly until the slope took control of the wagon's motion and let it tip over on to its wheels.

The wagon continued tipping until it stood at an angle looking as if it'd tumble down to the creek, but then it rocked back on to its wheels and shuddered to a halt.

Dalton patted the side and headed around to the front to examine the tongue while he put his mind to the problem of how he could fashion a collar and harness.

'You should have planned this better,' a man said behind him, making Dalton turn.

While he'd been preoccupied, three riders had crested the rise. One man had moved ahead of the others and was considering Dalton sceptically.

'I couldn't plan anything,' Dalton said lightly. 'My name's Dalton and I'm heading to Lonetree. I never expected to come across this.'

'So whose wagon is it?' the man asked after revealing he was Remington Forsyth and his companions were the Broughton brothers, Lawrence and Hamilton. 'Where's the owner gone? What are you—?'

'I told you: I saw smoke and so I investigated.'

Remington dismissed Dalton's protestations of innocence with a sorry shake of the head before turning to the other two men.

'I haven't got the time to listen to stories. Find out what he was really doing while I head inland.'

As Remington moved off at a gallop, Dalton returned to checking out his lucky find, but following Remington's orders, Lawrence positioned himself between Dalton and the creek while

Hamilton rode around the wagon.

With these men being suspicious of his actions, Dalton moved casually towards his horse, but this encouraged the brothers to dismount, ensuring that no matter which way he turned one of them could block him.

'I told you the truth,' Dalton said, backing away while raising his hands. 'I don't want no trouble.'

His movement made Lawrence glance at Dalton's leg for the first time and note the ponderous way he walked. A glimmer of doubt, presumably about Dalton's actions, flashed in his eyes, but it came too late to stop Hamilton from moving in.

Hamilton tried to grab him from behind, but before he could lay a hand on him, Dalton pivoted on his good leg. He used his momentum to slap a straight-armed blow using the flat of his hand against his opponent's cheek, sending him reeling away.

Then he turned to confront Lawrence, but while he'd been tussling, this man had moved out of view. Dalton struggled to turn and seek him out.

So he was looking at Hamilton when a shadow moved on the ground and alerted him a moment before Lawrence leapt out from behind the wagon. He caught Dalton around the shoulders and knocked him over on to his chest.

Quick blows rained down on his back and sides. Then Hamilton joined his brother and knelt on the small of Dalton's back, pinning him to the ground.

It had been a while since Dalton had broken his leg and so jolts no longer pained him, but he still had only limited strength in the leg and so he floundered. After struggling to raise himself with his good leg, he went limp, hoping to make his attackers underestimate him.

This failed as Lawrence dragged his arms behind his back and Hamilton drew him up to a standing position. Dalton didn't fight back, maintaining the subterfuge of being weak.

'We want the truth,' Hamilton said. 'What happened here?'

'I don't know,' Dalton said, with as much calmness as he could muster. 'I was heading to Lonetree when I found this wagon lying on its side.'

Hamilton looked at Lawrence, who snorted.

'I don't believe him,' he said. 'He hasn't got a leg to stand on.'

Both his opponents sniggered and so Dalton uttered a rueful laugh, but that made Hamilton sneer.

'You reckon stealing is funny, do you?' he muttered.

'I only righted it. Without me doing so, it'd have probably rolled down into the water and been lost.'

Hamilton raised an eyebrow, as if something Dalton had said had interested him and he glanced at Lawrence. They both chuckled, confirming they were of the same mind. They made Dalton struggle, but he couldn't dislodge his captors.

He was bent double, turned towards the wagon, and then they ran him towards it. At the last moment he averted his face, but his right cheek and shoulder still mashed into the side of the wagon, making it creak.

He tried to shake off the blow, but that had the unfortunate effect of making him raise his forehead as he was dashed against the side for a second time. The blow cracked a plank and the noise reverberated in Dalton's head as his vision dimmed and his limbs went limp.

He slumped in his captors' grip and, when they dashed him against the side for a third time, it was as if the collision had happened to someone else.

They continued manhandling him roughly; Dalton struggled to focus on what their intentions were as they walked him on and dragged him off the ground while holding only his arms.

He must have blacked out as it came as a shock when he found he was no longer being held. He was lying on his chest with rough wood beneath him and so he flexed his muscles as he gathered his strength before fighting back.

A thud sounded, adding urgency to his need to move. He sat up and found he'd been placed in the wagon. Through the burnt away section of canvas, the sky was moving and, as he was being jiggled, he struggled to sit upright.

He presumed he was being taken somewhere, but when he shuffled round to face the front, nobody was on the seat. The creek was ahead. And it was getting closer at an alarming rate.

He dragged himself towards the seat, by which time he'd confirmed the men had turned the wagon to the creek and shoved it on its way. The wheels were protesting loudly as they trundled over every rock in their path.

Each obstacle jolted Dalton up into the air making it clear he wouldn't be able to climb on to the seat. So he grabbed the side as he sought to leave by the quickest way possible.

From the corner of his eye he saw only the roiling water as he pulled himself up to the sideboard. Then a crunch sounded, the noise as loud as what Dalton would expect from the wagon hitting the ground rather than water.

He was torn away from the side and, unable to control his motion, he rolled head over heels to the front of the wagon where he tipped over the seat and hit the water flat on his back.

Within moments the creek swallowed him up and, as he'd not had enough time to gather his breath, he waved his arms frantically as he sought to reach the surface.

The strong current tore at him, tipping him over and drawing him along, but to his relief in the water he was less incapacitated than on land and he was able to use both legs.

Two kicks brought him to the surface where he faced the river-bank that seemed to be surging along only a body's length from his hands.

The cold water revived his senses as he kicked towards the bank, but he didn't move any closer and, after another three kicks, he had to admit the bank might as well be a mile away.

Worse, the current dragged him down and he had to use all his energy to thrust his head back above water. While he could still breathe, he gathered a lungful of air and, to rest his previously injured leg, he swam using only his arms as he sought to propel himself to the bank.

He didn't feel he was making any progress, but then darkness swept over him a moment before a prominent length of bank that jutted into the creek loomed above him. The current sought to swirl him past the headland, but Dalton reckoned this was his best chance and he dove down through the current.

He managed one forward stroke using his arms. Then his grasping hands clawed against the muddy ground beneath the water.

When he came up, he was pressed flat against the slick bank while the water sluiced over him, threatening to drag him away. Dalton scrambled a hand against the ground and found purchase.

Then he strained to raise his other hand up as far as he was able. His fingers clamped around rotting vegetation and when he tugged, he found enough resistance to let him claw his way higher.

It took him a minute to drag himself only a foot

out of the water, but even as his strength gave out, his movements became easier as more of his body emerged from the fierce current. Inch by inch he drew himself on until his legs came free and he was able to flop down on his chest on the ground.

He looked up, seeing his tormentors cresting the rise. They had their backs to him and, to Dalton's relief, they didn't look back as they disappeared from view.

He confirmed he was several feet above water level while the wagon that had started his troubles was a dozen feet out into the creek. Then it slid beneath the surface with a sucking noise that sounded like a sigh.

When Dalton stood up and saw his horse had been run off, he sighed too.

Lights were illuminating the evening sky when Dalton first saw Lonetree. The sight didn't cheer him, though, as his tormentors had ridden this way.

Although the late afternoon sun had dried his clothes, the last few hours had been annoying. He'd not had to walk for any distance on his injured leg before and so it had taken him three hours to catch his spooked horse.

The town overlooked Black Creek and nestled at the base of a hill on which stood a large and solitary dead oak. Dalton rode down the hill and, after passing a saloon, he veered towards a stable, but he stopped when he saw the sign above the door that showed that it was owned by the Broughton brothers.

He was too tired for a confrontation and so he searched for a law office instead, which he located two buildings down from the stable. When he headed into the office, the room was quiet.

The town marshal, Virgil Greeley, sat behind his desk facing the door with his feet up, his arms folded and his hat drawn down over his eyes.

'What do you want?' Greeley asked with bored indifference without raising his hat.

'I'm here to report a crime,' Dalton said.

This declaration did made Greeley raise his hat. He was portly with an unkempt beard that sparsely covered his sagging jowls, but his eyes were lively.

'Now that sure is interesting. What crime are you talking about?'

His raised voice made a man look in from an adjoining office. For several seconds he and Dalton stared at each other in surprise until with a narrow-eyed glare Dalton acknowledged they'd met upriver.

'I reckon you already know.' Dalton pointed at the newcomer. 'That man Remington told the Broughton brothers to question me, but they attacked me instead.'

While Remington came in and leaned against the wall to consider him, Greeley shook his head.

'Remington's my deputy.' He raised an eyebrow. 'So do you want to take back that accusation or shall I throw you in a cell?'

CHAPTER 2

'I'm not accusing Remington,' Dalton said, meeting Greeley's eye. 'I am accusing the Broughton brothers.'

Remington walked across the law office to stand before Dalton.

'You were acting suspiciously and so I left them to question you rigorously,' he said. 'When they returned to town, they told me you'd done nothing wrong. That ought to end the matter.'

'It would, except they decided to have some fun by throwing me in the wagon and rolling it into the creek. I barely got out of the water alive.'

Remington winced, the brothers' actions clearly not being his intent, but he said nothing as he let Greeley adjudicate. The marshal considered Remington, which made his deputy gulp.

'See the brothers and sort this out,' Greeley said, standing up. 'The days when Lonetree tolerated the behaviour of men like Judah Sundown and the Broughton brothers has passed. Any deputy of mine must be seen to uphold the law, not excuse the men who break it.'

Remington was half the marshal's age and a head taller, and so the rebuke made him rock back and forth on his toes until, with an aggrieved grunt, he turned to the door.

'Obliged you believed me,' Dalton said when Remington had slammed the door shut.

'I didn't say that,' Greeley said as he came round his desk. 'That was between me and my deputy.'

'Either way I told the truth.' Dalton watched Greeley raise an eyebrow as if he expected him to say more, and so Dalton shrugged. 'I assume you know whose wagon it was.'

Greeley grunted, suggesting he had wanted to hear that response.

'I do.' He gestured at the door. 'You'll need somewhere to stay tonight. I'll show you to a decent place.'

Dalton didn't press for details and Greeley didn't provide any, but the marshal was as good as his word as the Culver Hotel's rooms were cheap and clean.

Before finding the wagon, Dalton had been undecided whether to cross Black Creek at Harmison's Ford or to move on to Wilson's Crossing. Either way, he had enough money to loiter on the east side of the water for several weeks, even if he couldn't find work.

When Dalton had eaten and rested up in his room, the lively sounds coming from the First Star saloon down the main drag encouraged him to put aside his anger. He stood at the window and, after watching Lonetree at night for half an hour, he saw no reason to change his plan.

Once he'd enjoyed a few nights in the saloon, he doubted he'd find work or anything to occupy his time in such a small settlement.

He was returning to his bed when the hotel owner Marietta Culver knocked on his door. She was tall with a long neck and a penetrating gaze.

'Marshal Greeley told me,' she said, her voice authoritative but harsh with emotion, 'that you found my daughter Sera's wagon upriver.'

Dalton nodded and offered a smile. 'You don't look old enough to have a daughter.'

'I'm not in the mood for compliments and before you ask, I've yet to be married.'

She gave him a stern look, suggesting she often had to explain this matter and so Dalton returned a concerned expression.

'I hope Sera's fine.'

Marietta frowned, but when he levered himself into a chair awkwardly, she considered his leg. Then, using matter-of-fact movements, she examined his splints before suggesting he should raise his leg. She sat on another chair facing him.

'Nobody has seen her since she left town this morning,' she said, while moving buckles and

17

tightening straps. 'Did you see her?'

'I was heading downriver and I saw nobody.'

'I was told the wagon was on fire.'

She had been making the splints feel more comfortable, but while making her last comment she tugged a strap and so Dalton spoke lightly.

'It was a small fire, and it didn't look as if it had been lit with sinister intent.' He looked her in the eye until she nodded. 'And the fire meant the wagon couldn't have been abandoned for long. So she can't have strayed far.'

'Deputy Forsyth headed upriver and said he saw nobody.' She stopped work to consider. 'With you coming downriver, that means she went inland. I'll make sure tomorrow's search concentrates there.'

Her clipped tone said that despite her comment, she knew Sera could have gone in the only direction they hadn't mentioned.

He gestured at his leg. 'You know what you're doing.'

'I do.'

She leaned back and signalled that he should stand. To his delight, she'd made his splints more supportive than they'd ever been.

'You do.' He smiled, although she didn't return it.

She bustled to the door, but when she'd opened it, she stopped and then turned back.

'I get the impression you know what you're doing too.'

'I'm looking for work, if that's what you mean.'

Dalton stood tall, appearing as presentable as he could. 'And I can turn my hand to most things.'

'Would that include finding a missing person?'

'I've never done anything like that before, but I'd like to help in any way I can.'

'I appreciate your honesty, and I was impressed that your summary conveyed more information and concern than Marshal Greeley managed. If I leave it to him to find Sera, I may never see her again.'

Dalton patted his leg. 'This constrains what I can do.'

'On the other hand, it'll ensure you're thorough. I'll pay a dollar a day plus expenses and each evening I'll help you exercise your leg to aid your recovery. I intend to offer a reward for my daughter's safe return and so if you find her, I'll pay whatever you ask.'

'I accept.' He waited until she nodded and then raised a hand. 'But it sounds as if you expect this search will take a while. So tell me what I need to know.'

She gestured at the window, signifying the whole town.

'I'm a wealthy woman living in a small town with a daughter and no husband, so I wasn't surprised when I received an anonymous, threatening letter demanding money. I didn't let that change my behaviour, so when Sera wanted to go upriver to paint I let her. When she was late back, Deputy Forsyth recruited the Broughton—'

'They'd be the last men I'd turn to for help,' Dalton spluttered, unable to keep his silence.

She frowned. 'I agree, but Deputy Forsyth reckoned he could keep them in line and I trust him.'

Dalton didn't want to mention that the deputy had failed and, when footfalls sounded in the corridor, he provided an encouraging nod.

Deputy Forsyth arrived making Marietta smile for the first time that Dalton had seen. He and Marietta embraced before Marietta left, having promised to see Remington in her quarters when he'd finished speaking with Dalton.

'Did you sort out the Broughton brothers?' Dalton said when her footfalls reached the stairs.

'As best as I could. I need all the assistance I can get, so I can't refuse their help, but I'm sorry for what happened upriver.'

Remington raised an eyebrow and Dalton nodded, accepting his apology.

'I understand. We must all put aside our differences until Sera is safe.'

'And either way, I'm keen to resolve this problem quickly; once I've sorted out this mess Marietta and I are to be wed.'

'I was once a contented married man and so I'll do my best to ensure you're wed quickly.' Dalton gestured at the door. 'She's hired me to find Sera.'

Remington tipped back his hat in surprise.

'Then I hope you won't be employed for long, as I intend to find her before you can hobble out of this room.'

Dalton laughed. 'I hope you can.'

'In case I don't, remember this: despite what I told the brothers, they aren't the sort to listen to advice, so while you're looking for Sera, look out for them.'

It was mid-morning when Dalton rode out of town. Earlier, Remington had instructed him to search downriver, even though that might give Marietta the answer she didn't want, while he concentrated his search upriver.

As he rode, Dalton examined the creek for areas where a body might wash up. Remington wanted him to go to Harmison's Ford, as someone there might have seen a body floating by, but after thirty minutes his heart thudded with concern.

Ahead was a bridge that crossed a tributary at Morgan's Gap. The Broughton brothers were at the riverside. They were too far away for him to work out what they were doing, but their hunched postures suggested they were concerned.

He veered down to the water, but his worst fears didn't materialize as they had found a washed-up wagon, presumably the one they'd rolled into the creek the day before. It had become moored in shallow water and they were struggling to draw in a rope they'd wrapped around the anchor.

Their muddied forms suggested they'd been unsuccessful and so Dalton drew to a halt, anticipating entertainment.

His hopes were dashed when the wagon surged clear of the mud and rolled on to dry land. Then Lawrence looked into the wagon and summoned Hamilton's attention.

When Dalton had been bundled into the back, the wagon had been empty, and so he was surprised when they dragged a sack over the side. As they dropped the sack on the ground, he moved closer.

His approach attracted the men's attention. They swung round to face him, their quick reactions making them appear guilty even though Dalton had seen them discover the sack.

They advanced, drawing their guns, making Dalton raise a hand, but they ignored his friendly gesture and fired. The shots were high and intended to warn him off, but unlike yesterday, Dalton didn't stay to explain himself and he tore the reins to the side and beat a hasty retreat back up the slope.

Two more gunshots hurried him on his way and both shots landed close enough for him to see dirt kick. When he looked over his shoulder, the brothers were gaining their horses.

Dalton didn't look back again as he moved up the rise. They could intercept him if he went for the bridge and so he turned back to town.

Five minutes passed before more high gunfire ripped out, this time accompanied by lively whoops as the brothers enjoyed the chase. When he looked back, his pursuers were cresting the rise, but they were now three hundred yards away.

Dalton concentrated on riding until he was halfway back to town, where irritation at the brothers' behaviour made him stop and then head for a tangle of boulders. Before he reached the rocks, he dismounted and sought refuge behind a mound.

He lay on his chest where he could see for a hundred yards ahead. The sloping terrain kept his pursuers out of sight, but they had been on his tail and so he expected them to appear at any moment.

After two minutes they hadn't arrived and so Dalton raised himself, wondering if they'd carried on to town. When he could see the creek, the two men were still not visible and so, feeling vulnerable, he moved out from the boulders just as he saw movement to his right.

He turned, seeing a shadow flitter on the ground from one of the men having taken a roundabout route to sneak up on him. Dalton had yet to see the other man and so, hobbling as quickly as he was able, he reached the boulder and pressed his back to the rock.

When he heard nothing, he swung round the boulder and met Lawrence edging forward with both hands raised ready to grab him. The two men stared at each other from only two feet apart.

Dalton got over his surprise first and he swung up his fist catching Lawrence with a backhanded blow beneath the chin that cracked his head back and sent him reeling into the boulder. Lawrence rebounded and walked into a punch to the stomach that bent him double before with his good leg, Dalton kicked his legs from under him.

'That's for knocking me into the wagon,' he muttered. He dragged Lawrence to his feet and, while he was still bent double, he turned him to the creek and threw him to the ground. 'And that's for rolling me into the water.'

Lawrence tumbled to the ground and rolled down a slope before he shuddered to a halt in a cloud of dust. He wasted no time in getting up on his haunches to face Dalton.

'You won't collect the reward,' Lawrence muttered.

'I'll get paid no matter who finds Sera.' Dalton watched Lawrence wince, confirming they hadn't been offered the same deal. 'What was in the sack you found?'

Dalton didn't expect an answer, but Lawrence shifted his weight and turned slightly away from him.

'We left it for Remington to examine.'

Dalton nodded, for the first time thinking that these men might have Sera's best interests in mind, even if it was only to claim the reward. But Lawrence used his momentary lapse in concentration to leap aside and roll out of sight.

Dalton backed away and his retreat had a second benefit when a shadow moved and alerted him to the fact that Hamilton had been sneaking up on him.

He hopped aside as Hamilton leapt from the boulder behind him, his action letting Hamilton crash down on his feet without touching him before pitching forward on to his knees. Dalton took advantage and delivered a swiping punch to the back of Hamilton's neck, sending him sprawling on to his chest.

Dalton planted his good foot on Hamilton's right shoulder blade, pinning him down. A moment later Lawrence arrived, his eager grin that anticipated Hamilton's success turning to a scowl when he saw that Dalton was in control.

'We're even now,' Dalton said. He waited, but neither man answered and so he pressed down, making Hamilton grunt. 'We both want Sera's safe return, so I suggest we spend our time finding her instead of feuding.'

Lawrence's right eye twitched, but Hamilton bleated a warning for him to comply, the ground masking his words.

'And I suggest,' Lawrence said, 'the moment we find her you leave town quickly.'

Reckoning this was the best reconciliation they could manage, Dalton raised his foot and Hamilton wasted no time in rolling away and getting up.

Hamilton joined Lawrence and the two men backed away. Dalton let them leave unchallenged while shaking his head in bemusement at their behaviour.

When he was sure they were leaving, he headed to

his horse. He resumed his journey downriver except now, with the wagon having washed up, the thought of what else he might find filled him with dread.

'You were hungry,' Marietta said.

'It's been a long day,' Dalton said. He pushed his empty plate away and sat back from the table. 'But not a productive one.'

She nodded and drew up a chair to join him in the hotel dining room. She signified he should raise his leg so she could check his straps.

Dalton's journey to Harmison's Ford had been a fruitless one and the return trip had been tiring. He rested his leg on a spare chair and watched Marietta while she worked. Her worried expression confirmed that Sera hadn't been found yet.

Dalton searched for the right words to explain what he'd seen earlier, but Remington arrived and resolved his dilemma. He leaned against the doorframe with his expression stern.

'It's too dark to continue searching,' he said to Marietta, his sombre tone providing a summary of his progress and making Marietta lower her head.

'Have you talked with the Broughton brothers yet?' Dalton asked.

Remington headed across the room to face Dalton.

'They showed me the sack they'd found on the wagon, and it makes this situation even worse.'

'How?' Marietta asked with a gulp.

'Sera has been kidnapped,' Remington said, placing a hand on her shoulder. 'A ransom demand was in the sack. You must pay five thousand dollars before sundown tomorrow or Sera dies.'

CHAPTER 3

The meeting had lasted for an hour, but so far nobody had offered any good ideas.

Marietta had gathered everyone involved in the search into the hotel dining room to debate what she should do the following day.

Marshal Greeley sat behind a table at the front of the room with Deputy Forsyth who had gone through the incident from the beginning. With the Broughton brothers sitting on one side of the room, Dalton had sat with Marietta on the other side.

Although the marshal's meticulous manner made Lawrence and Hamilton smirk at each other, neither man gave any outward recognition of the incident downriver. So Dalton hoped they'd honour their agreement.

The tales they and Deputy Forsyth told were similar. They had visited several places without finding any clues as to where Sera had been taken and they had spoken with numerous people without gaining any information on who might have kidnapped her.

Unlike the others, Dalton welcomed hearing the slow relating of events as it filled in the details he'd missed, even if they didn't give him any ideas. Sundown was approaching when the marshal turned to him to explain what he'd discovered that day.

'Nothing,' Hamilton said before Dalton could reply, making Lawrence laugh, although they were silenced when Remington glared at them.

'That sums it up,' Dalton said levelly. 'I know nothing and I found out nothing.'

'Even so,' Greeley persisted, 'take me through what you—'

'We haven't got the time,' Dalton said. 'You have less than a day to find Sera and sitting around here talking won't find her.'

'I agree with Dalton,' Remington said, punching a fist into a palm with a resounding slap. 'We should back our best hunch.'

Greeley considered Remington with irritation.

'So,' Greeley said, sitting back in his chair, 'impress me with your hunch.'

Remington took a deep breath, although his uncertain gaze suggested he couldn't offer a viable course of action, but he didn't get to speak as a steady tapping started up.

The noise continued until everyone turned to Marietta, who was rapping a coin on her chair arm.

'I've heard enough,' she said. 'We won't sit around

talking any more, but neither will we back any hunches. I'll pay the ransom.'

'But you can't,' Remington murmured, aghast. 'That'll take every cent you have.'

'The kidnappers are threatening to take every member of family I have.'

Remington opened and closed his mouth, seemingly lost for words, leaving Marshal Greeley to speak up.

'My deputy's right. If you relent, the future will be bleak for anyone who has money.'

'Dealing with such problems,' Marietta said levelly, 'is your responsibility. As you've failed, I have to do what I feel is right. This discussion is over and we'll now decide how I can fulfil the kidnappers' demand.'

'They've specified the place and the procedure.' Greeley stood up and collected his notes into a pile. 'I suggest you make your own arrangements to comply with them.'

'I thought you'd help.'

'You thought wrong. I won't support a criminal act.' He turned to Remington. 'It's time for us to leave. We've neglected our other duties for too long.'

Remington stood up before with a visible wrench he appeared to register what he'd been ordered to do.

'I can't go,' he said. 'I have to help Marietta sort this out.'

'I can't accept a deputy who doesn't follow my orders.'

Remington glared at Greeley as he considered the obvious ultimatum. Dalton reckoned Remington's firm-set jaw meant he'd defy him, but Marietta spoke up first.

'Go with the marshal,' she said. 'If a lawman gets involved, the kidnappers will react badly.'

'You're right.' Remington sneered at Greeley. 'So I resign, which means I'm free to deal with this.'

Greeley accepted his decision without a flicker of concern. He tucked his notes under his arm and left the room, leaving Remington to gesture at the other men to join him.

While Remington conferred with the brothers, Dalton dallied to speak with Marietta.

'If it helps,' he said. 'I reckon Remington made the right choice.'

'In defying Greeley, yes,' Marietta said, 'but not in accepting assistance from Lawrence and Hamilton. Remington has known them for a long time and so he would never admit it, but he needs help to keep them in line. I'd like you to go with them and watch his back.'

'The brothers are sure to hate that.' Dalton winked. 'So I'd be delighted to go.'

It was dark when the covered wagon that would deliver the ransom was ready to roll out of town. They would use the dried-out and repaired wagon that had been dragged out of the water earlier.

The exchange of money for Marietta's daughter would take place on a ridge in High Pass.

The kidnappers had chosen this location well, as it was a day's journey away, forcing the group to ride for several hours that night before embarking on another long journey the following day to meet the sundown deadline.

The urgency of the situation made everyone move quickly and without rancour. When Dalton offered to drive the wagon, nobody complained.

He took the wagon behind the hotel, after which Lawrence and Hamilton carried a large box outside and deposited it on the wagon. Dalton was surprised Marietta had raised the money so quickly and Remington was edgy, but with a shrug he appeared to dismiss the matter.

'I don't care about the money,' Marietta said, addressing the four men. 'Sera's life is all that matters. Promise me you'll take no risks.'

She waited until all four men had provided solemn pledges after which she asked them to bow their heads while she murmured a prayer. Then she dismissed them and in short order the men mounted up.

As Dalton moved off, Lawrence and Hamilton flanked the wagon while Remington stayed behind to speak with Marietta before he hurried on to join them. Then, at a steady mile-eating pace, they trundled into the darkness.

Remington rode ahead of the wagon, which was fine with Dalton, as he was unsure of the route. Lawrence and Hamilton dropped back to check nobody had followed them out of town, but after an hour they accepted they hadn't attracted any unwanted attention.

They rode for several more hours without incident until Remington called a halt.

Dalton judged it was about midnight and Remington chose a high point where they could see in all directions. The only shelter they could find from a brisk wind was in a hollow.

Remington didn't want to attract attention with a fire, even if they could find something to burn. So he and Dalton hunched up on one side of the hollow to take the first watch while Lawrence and Hamilton rested.

They aimed to swap watches in the middle of the night and move on at first light.

Despite the need to be vigilant, Dalton struggled to concentrate on the bleak, moonlit landscape and so before long he stood up to stretch his aching leg.

'How did you break your leg?' Remington asked.

'I'd always wondered whether falling fifty feet on to rocky ground would hurt.' Dalton smiled. 'So I tried it. And it did.'

'At least you now know,' Remington laughed before assuming a serious expression. 'It won't stop you taking a full part in tomorrow's exchange, will it?'

Dalton glanced at the Broughton brothers. They were awake and listening to their conversation while sporting smirks that suggested they were waiting for an opportunity to butt in and find fault with him.

'No. I'll do whatever you need me to.'

'That shouldn't be much other than to stay back and look out for deception. I'll complete the transfer.'

'After that, you can't return to your old job, so what will you do?'

'Being a deputy marshal was a temporary position. I only accepted it to prove to Marietta I could do more than tend bar. When we have Sera back, I'll work with Marietta to restore her . . . our fortunes.'

'I'm surprised she raised the money in a few hours.'

Remington frowned at Dalton's obvious attempt to dig for information, confirming that back in town he had been surprised too.

'That's not sinister. She's a wealthy woman.'

'It might not be sinister on her part, but the kidnappers gave her little time to pay up, so they must have known she had the funds available.'

Remington nodded slowly as if he'd not considered this possibility, his silence giving Lawrence a chance to speak up for the first time.

'If we're careful,' he said with a significant glance at the wagon and then his gun, 'you might not have to restore your fortunes.'

Remington pointed a firm finger at Lawrence.

'We promised Marietta we'd take no risks and I don't want to bring Sera back lying in that box.'

Lawrence sneered, but didn't reply. Hamilton stood and took a slow walk around the hollow.

'I know a better way to fill the box,' he said as he stopped behind Dalton, making him turn.

Hamilton's grin was bright in the low moonlight, alerting Dalton to what he intended to do and so he was on guard when Hamilton kicked out.

Dalton caught Hamilton's ankle while the rising boot was still six inches from his face and then twisted it while shoving it aside. His action made Hamilton stumble and, off-balance, he tumbled into the hollow.

Before he could get his wits about him, Dalton shuffled towards him. Then, using his good leg, he kicked off and leapt on Hamilton's back.

He settled his weight on his shoulders and shoved his face into the dirt. Then he looked for Lawrence, but Lawrence had raised his hands while backing away, although that was only because Remington had drawn a gun on him.

'I told you,' Remington muttered, 'I aim to complete this mission without mishaps. I don't want you two slugging it out with Dalton for the next day.'

'Then get rid of the problem,' Lawrence said, his demand making Hamilton stop struggling as he awaited a verdict that, if he could see Remington's stern expression, he would be able to guess.

'I would,' Remington said levelly, 'if I didn't need

three men in case tomorrow doesn't go according to plan.'

'We three can deal with anything.'

'I meant that two men won't be enough.'

Lawrence drew in his breath sharply and the two men faced each other until Lawrence relented with a snorted laugh. When Remington glanced at Dalton, he clambered off Hamilton, who joined Lawrence without meeting his eye.

With there being nothing else to say on the matter, they returned to their previous arrangement of Remington and Dalton sitting on one side of the hollow and the Broughton brothers sitting on the other.

Before long, the brothers dozed and so Dalton and Remington stayed quiet.

Dalton judged the passing of time by the moon's slow passage across the night sky and, when he reckoned half the night had gone, Remington woke up the others.

Nobody spoke as the brothers started their watch, giving Dalton hope that the disagreements had finally been resolved. Either way, he was so tired he went to sleep quickly.

Seemingly, only moments later Remington shook his shoulder. When he stirred and looked around, it was lighter.

'I could have done with a few more minutes,' Dalton said around a yawn before he noted Remington's irritated expression. 'What's wrong?'

'It's the Broughton brothers,' Remington said. 'They've gone. It seems my ultimatum was too. . . .'

Remington trailed off and swung round to face the wagon, his concerned expression showing he'd had the same worrying thought that had just hit Dalton.

'No matter how heavily we slept,' Dalton said, as Remington hurried to the wagon and peered into the back, 'they still left quietly. Surely they couldn't have taken the ransom money.'

Remington's eyes narrowed as, with a gulp, he clambered into the wagon.

Dalton reached the back as Remington moved the lid from the box. The ease with which he shoved it aside showed it hadn't been secured well and when he slapped a hand to his brow, Dalton provided a sympathetic groan.

'They've stolen the ransom,' Remington murmured, 'and condemned Sera to death.'

CHAPTER 4

'Marietta was worried about the brothers,' Dalton said, 'and she had good cause. You sided with me and they reacted badly.'

Remington nodded and kicked the box, making it tip over, and confirmed it was empty before he jumped down. He looked back towards Lonetree.

'I've known them for years. I gave them the benefit of the doubt and thought I could control them, but clearly I was wrong.'

'You made a mistake, but we can't afford to waste time.' Dalton slapped his arm to encourage him to think positively, but that proved to be the wrong thing to do as Remington bunched a fist. Then, with an angry oath he punched the wood beside Dalton's shoulder before storming away to stand hunched over.

This time Dalton let him calm down naturally.

After a while, his voice still strained, Remington said, 'Go back to town, find them and reclaim the ransom money, or meet the deadline?'

'The exchange is in twelve hours and we face a journey of ten hours, so that's not enough time to find the brothers and, if we go back to town, we'll miss the deadline. But meeting that deadline won't help Sera, so we need another option.'

By way of an explanation Dalton glanced at his gun, but Remington shook his head.

'We do what Marietta would want us to do, which doesn't involve ambushing the kidnappers and risking Sera's life. We meet the deadline and try to explain ourselves so we can buy us enough time to put this right.'

Dalton didn't agree with this plan, but as Remington was in charge, he provided a sharp nod and without further comment, headed to the wagon. Remington mounted up and so, as they had done the previous day, they rode on with Remington leading.

Remington sat in the saddle with his head lowered, clearly lost in thought. So Dalton used the journey to consider plans, but as he couldn't envisage the situation they'd face, he couldn't think of a course of action other than to follow Remington's lead.

At noon they reached the entrance to High Pass. An hour after that they climbed to higher ground, which they spent the rest of the afternoon traversing.

When the sun was approaching the distant horizon, Remington stopped and pointed out the ridge where the transfer would take place.

Even from several miles away, Dalton could see the kidnappers had chosen the location well. The ridge was a narrow passageway between two high points, with the steep sides comprising of loose rocks that would be difficult to climb.

The high point would let the kidnappers see for miles in all directions and ensure it would be hard to sneak up on them unobserved. So they rode openly, reaching the end of the ridge while the sun was still an outstretched hand's width above the horizon.

Both men dismounted and stood back to back to observe all directions from which they could be approached. Fifty yards to Dalton's left the rocky ground sloped away, while to his right an overhang provided cover for anyone who might be watching them.

In this exposed place, he and Remington would struggle to defend themselves and so, with no movement and no noise other than the breeze rustling by, time passed slowly.

'Have you known Marietta long?' Dalton asked after a while.

'I used to tend bar in the First Star and she often visited the owner, Edwidge Star. We got talking and things have gone well from there. I've grown to care for Sera too, which is important.'

Dalton rocked his head from side to side before he asked the question he couldn't help but wonder about.

'Who was Sera's father?'

Remington frowned. 'Marietta made it clear she won't answer that question. I suggest after we've got Sera back, you don't ask her either.'

Dalton nodded after which he was content to remain silent. The sun had grown large and red when Remington got his attention and pointed across the pass. On the high point opposite, people were making their way down towards the ridge.

Dalton counted six people. By the time they were the same distance from the ridge as he and Remington were, he discerned that one person was being secured by two others.

'We're facing five men,' Dalton said, edging closer to Remington.

'Which is too many if you're still thinking about trying something.' Remington gestured at the overhang. 'And others are sure to be hiding up there.'

'Someone could be, but I haven't seen anyone yet.' Dalton raised a hand when Remington started to retort. 'But you're in charge and if you want to argue this out with the kidnappers, that's what we'll do.'

'Obliged. We do nothing that'll jeopardize Sera's life.'

Remington moved away and Dalton fell in behind him. Loose stones covered the ridge ensuring that Dalton found the going slow. So when Remington stopped a third of the way across the ridge he was well ahead of him.

Only then did the people on the opposite side

move towards them. In keeping with Dalton's earlier observation, three men walked at the front while the other two walked behind, each man holding the arms of what he could now see was a young woman.

As Remington had done, the lead group stopped a third of a way on to the ridge, arriving at that point as Dalton reached Remington. This left them fifty yards apart where they stood watching each other.

'Do you recognize them?' Dalton asked.

When Remington didn't reply immediately, he repeated his question and that made Remington shake himself before with a gruff voice he replied.

'The lead man is Judah Sundown. He used to sort out trouble in the First Star.'

'And the others?'

'I don't recognize them, but before Edwidge ran him out of town, the saloon attracted plenty of rowdy men. I'd guess he's recruited help from amongst them.'

'Why did Edwidge get rid of him?'

'Judah's method of controlling customers was brutal and so last year Edwidge finally stood up to him, while Marshal Greeley said he'd shoot him on sight if he ever showed his face in Lonetree again.'

'It sounds as if Judah might have a grudge against Edwidge and the marshal, so why has he kidnapped Marietta's daughter?'

'I don't know.' Remington glanced at the low sun and forced a thin smile. 'Perhaps one of us should have realized Judah was behind this, as he used to live up to his name by setting ultimatums that expired at sundown; they used to call him the Sundown Kid.'

'He looks too old to be called that, but it makes this situation even more dangerous.'

Remington nodded and edged from side to side as he waited for Judah to make the first move, but as time dragged on without Judah delivering instructions, he became more agitated and glanced over his shoulder. He winced, making Dalton turn and see that their earlier guess had been correct.

At least five men were clambering down the overhang. When the leading man reached flat ground, he walked purposefully towards their wagon at a pace that within the next minute would uncover that they didn't have the ransom money.

'I guess,' Remington said, 'it's time to explain.'

'Be convincing,' Dalton said, gathering a stern nod from Remington before he moved off.

Dalton had started to move when Judah raised a hand.

'No further, Remington,' he shouted. 'Until I have the money, you stay where we can all see you.'

Remington kept walking although he spread his hands wide apart, and so Dalton followed.

'We need to discuss the ransom,' Remington shouted. 'There's—'

'No talk. No tricks. No more steps.' Judah gestured at the men behind him. 'Unless you want to take a dead girl back to Lonetree.'

'That's not the deal,' Remington said, still walking. 'We give you money in exchange for Sera. If she's harmed in any way, you don't get your money.'

'It's too late to start making. . . .' Judah trailed off as he clearly noticed Remington's low tone. 'Are you going back on our deal?'

Judah's voice rose as he aimed an accusing finger at Remington, making him stop. Remington lowered his head and kicked at the rocks beneath his feet before he continued in a soft voice.

'There's been a problem. We need to talk.'

Judah gestured at the wagon and a few moments later someone shouted. While still moving on, Dalton glanced back at the man who was standing before the wagon and gesticulating with a clear signal that he'd searched the wagon and it was empty.

'You worked in the First Star and you know what I'm capable of,' Judah muttered. 'Yet still you defied me.'

'Wait!' Remington spluttered.

Judah's sneer said he wouldn't listen to reason and so when Dalton reached Remington, he stopped behind him and whispered urgently in his ear.

'We're exposed out here on the ridge with gunmen ahead of us and behind us,' he said. 'There's no way out of this for any of us unless you're more persuasive.'

Remington gulped as he considered Judah, the gunmen flanking him and the men holding Sera.

None of them moved, suggesting he was being given one last chance to state his case.

Remington opened and closed his mouth soundlessly as he clearly struggled to find the right words. Then he gave up trying and dropped to his knees where he raised his hands in a begging gesture.

'Take me as a hostage,' he screeched, his voice echoing in the pass, 'but don't harm her.'

Judah curled his upper lip in disgust and so Dalton decided he would have to do the talking instead. With Remington blocking Judah's view of his lower body, he drew his gun and, when nobody looked at him, he raised his gun arm to aim at Judah.

'Only one thing is certain here,' he declared as he stepped out from behind Remington, 'unless we come to a deal, the Sundown Kid won't see another sundown.'

Judah considered him for the first time.

'Shoot me and the rest will take you alive,' he said calmly. 'Your screams will—'

'Quit with the threats,' Dalton said, still moving forward. 'You gave Marietta only a few hours to gather more money than I've seen in my entire life. So the new deal is: we'll pay the ransom as agreed, but you'll give her enough time to collect it.'

'She has the money. I know.'

Dalton kept walking and didn't reply until he was twenty paces from Judah.

'How do you know that?'

'Edwidge Star never could keep a secret.'

'And how did Edwidge know Marietta had the money?' He walked on and when he didn't get a reply, he persisted. 'What's going on here?'

Judah narrowed his eyes, his clenched fists and hunched posture confirming something about this situation was amiss. But Dalton moved on, figuring he'd taken the initiative and now he had to see it through.

He watched Judah as well as the other gunmen while behind him, Remington finally responded to his actions by murmuring a plea for him to desist. When Dalton didn't stop, scraping sounded as Remington stood up and hurried after him.

Dalton glanced at Sera, offering her encouragement with a confident smile, but she was shaking too much to return his gaze. He stomped to a halt before Judah, who considered him with disdain.

'You've picked the wrong man to try this bluff with,' Judah muttered.

Judah raised his left hand. The action was clearly a pre-arranged signal as one of the men holding Sera swung her forward while the other man released her.

In a moment the man brought his gun up against the side of her head. Dalton saw the fear in the young woman's eyes and the intent in the gunman's posture, and so he jerked his gun arm to the side, but he wasn't quick enough to save her.

Sera struggled and was trying to tear herself free when the gunman fired. Blood splattered and she staggered away with a hand rising to her forehead.

Behind him Remington screeched in anguish and so Dalton fired, catching the gunman with a high shot to the chest that made him drop to his knees and topple over on to his back.

Dalton could only watch in horror as Sera took a faltering step towards the edge of the ridge before she tipped over to lie on her chest. She landed on loose rocks that shifted and made her slip over the side.

Dalton moved towards her while firing on the run. As the gunmen got their wits about them, he caught the second man who had been holding Sera with a deadly shot to the head.

His other shots were wild, as was the gunfire his opponents returned. When he went down on his good knee and turned at the hip, he saw why they had aimed poorly.

The gunmen were all towering above him. One gunman levelled his gun on him, but then he lowered his arm, as he appeared to rise even higher.

Only then did Dalton realize with a lurch that was both mental and physical that the ground beneath his feet was falling away. As the gunmen disappeared from view above him, he spread his arms, an action that unbalanced him and made him flop down on to his rump.

He landed on a flat rock that was skating down the side of the ridge. So Dalton did the only thing he could: he grabbed the rock with one hand and raised his injured leg high.

Ground level was several hundred feet below, but rising dust soon took that out of view. After sliding along with relative ease for a dozen heartbeats, the rock tipped up and bucked Dalton away.

With desperate lunges he searched for purchase amidst the shifting rocks. He failed to stop himself as everything he touched lacked resistance, leaving him thankful he was riding the cascade. Then, as suddenly as the rocks had moved him, he stopped.

Stones covered his lower body, but as he hadn't stopped due to anything he'd done he lay still, unwilling to risk starting a new cascade. He heard rocks grinding behind him, but the dust blocked his view of what was causing the slippage.

Through the noise, gunfire peppered, but it was some distance away while the crash of rock against rock became louder and closer. Then a wave of shifting stones shoved him aside, landing him on his chest where he slid downwards again.

To his right Remington shouted in panic suggesting he too had taken a tumble down the ridge, but Dalton put Remington's plight from his mind as he dug his hands into the stones and sought to still himself. This time, after sliding for a few dozen yards, he halted.

He rolled on to his back. When he confirmed he was unhurt, gingerly he raised himself to his feet.

As he moved off, he stumbled, but he was pleased his injured leg had survived the ordeal without incurring any further harm. He worked his way downwards by standing crouched over and walking crablike using short and stiff-legged steps.

With each step the dust cleared and, after a minute, he saw the ground below, which was now only fifty feet away with most of the route down being comprised of larger and more stable-looking stones.

Then he saw movement and when he stopped, the dust settled letting him see that Remington had reached the bottom.

He was coated in dust and he stood awkwardly. His posture was hunched and defeated, and after taking a few more paces, Dalton saw what had concerned him.

At Remington's feet lay the still and blooded form of Sera, the young woman they'd come here to rescue.

CHAPTER 5

'Is she dead?' Dalton asked while he was still ten yards away from Remington.

He didn't get a reply until he'd slid his way down to ground level and then it was accompanied by Remington advancing on him with his expression set in a snarl.

'Yeah,' he muttered. 'But they didn't kill her. You did!'

'I tried to save her.' Dalton backed away for a pace. 'You saw that.'

'I saw what happened. You ignored my order to stay calm and you took over the negotiation. That forced Judah to react.'

Dalton lowered his head, accepting that even if Remington's harsh claim had been spoken in anger to provoke him, he had failed.

'I had to step in because you weren't explaining the situation well.'

A gunshot blasted, making Dalton look up.

Remington was advancing on him and he hadn't fired. When another gunshot rattled, he looked over his shoulder.

This time he saw dust kick from a boulder ten yards away. He looked up at the ridge; at the top the surviving gunmen had grouped together to shoot at them.

From either side other men were hurrying to join them and so Dalton turned back to warn Remington only to walk into a scything blow to the jaw that sent him reeling before he fell over on to his back.

'It was a tough negotiation,' Remington roared, 'and it didn't get any easier after you drew a gun on the Sundown Kid.'

Dalton sighed, reckoning that anything he said would only annoy Remington more and so he pointed upwards.

His action was accompanied by a fortuitous, in the circumstance, sustained volley of gunfire that made Remington look up. His angry gaze didn't alter as he considered the Sundown Kid and, when Dalton sought cover, he didn't join him.

Dalton shuffled on to a large boulder that was high enough to shield him from the ridge and from where he peered around the side at the kidnappers. They were showing no sign of coming down and so he didn't waste bullets on speculative shots.

'Get over here,' he shouted at Remington. 'We still have a chance to escape.'

Remington stormed over to him and stood in clear

view from above with his fists bunched.

'So saving your own hide is all you care about, is it?'

'It's too late to help Marietta's daughter now, but Judah Sundown can't get away with what he did, and that goes for Lawrence and Hamilton too.'

Remington had been rocking back and forth on his toes looking as if he was going to hit him again, but Dalton's last comment made him look aloft. He nodded and looked around before snarling.

'What you did was bad, but what they did was worse.'

He turned on his heel and walked away from the ridge, encouraging the kidnappers to fire at him. Slugs sliced into the ground to either side of Remington, but none of the shots came within five feet of him and neither did they slow him down.

'Wait for me,' Dalton called after him. 'We'll have a better chance together.'

'Just be grateful I'm letting the Sundown Kid deal with you,' Remington shouted with a disdainful wave of the hand before he quickened his pace.

Even if Remington had walked at a normal speed, Dalton doubted he could keep pace with him and so he stayed behind his cover.

When Remington moved out of sight, Dalton considered his own retreat. The sun had set and the terrain was darkening, but if he waited for too long, Judah would be able to make his way down.

As he wasn't prepared to try Remington's anger-fuelled method of just walking away, while he waited for the lull in the firing to become permanent, he planned a route away from the ridge.

He picked out a cluster of boulders as his first target and, after waiting for another fifteen minutes, during which time no more gunfire sounded, he ran on. He adopted a hobbling gait with a short step on his injured leg and a longer leap with the other.

He'd managed twenty paces before he attracted gunfire, but unlike the gunshots that had been aimed at Remington, they were more accurate and the first two shots that rang out kicked dust only a few paces ahead of him.

Dalton looked up the ridge, worried that Judah was coming down, but in fact he was no longer visible and he appeared to have moved on. Then Dalton saw where the shooting had originated.

At the base of the ridge, two men had taken refuge in a hollow after, presumably, following Judah's orders to clamber down and finish him off.

They were too far away and too well embedded for Dalton to take them on and so he hurried on to the cluster of boulders. Several more shots sliced into the ground, each one thankfully landing further away as he gained distance from the shooters.

Dalton only slowed when he'd rounded a large boulder that would hide him from all directions. He considered the rocks until he saw a gap between two sheer-sided boulders, and then moved on.

He figured that if he tried to run, he'd move so slowly he would be hunted down easily and so he had to make a stand. So, when he reached the other side, he went right and tracked along the back of the boulder until he found a place where he could climb.

Even so, by the time he reached the summit, the men had followed him. They were loitering down below and discussing where he'd gone, letting Dalton learn that the two men's names were Ellison and Victor.

A moment after he got his first uninterrupted view of them, his movement caused them to look up at him. So Dalton dropped down on to his chest.

He snaked along to the right and, when he peered down, the men were hurriedly passing below him. Dalton levelled his six-shooter on the nearest man, Ellison, but the men reacted instantly.

Ellison moved towards the boulder and out of Dalton's sight while the trailing Victor drew his gun and fired up at Dalton without raising his head.

The shot still kicked into the lip of the rock a foot from Dalton's right hand making him jerk away. When he moved back, Dalton's chance had been lost as both men were no longer visible.

Dalton slapped the rock in irritation and then shuffled to the left to gain a different angle on the scene below.

He still couldn't see either man and so he craned his neck to peer down the side of the boulder. Ellison was below him and he'd already trained his gun upwards, thankfully at a point several feet to Dalton's side.

In the moment it took Ellison to aim at him Dalton darted back, and the action saved him from a slug that clipped the edge of the rock. He waited for four heartbeats and swung his arm over the edge.

He fired blindly three times, splaying his shots to either side. Then he shuffled along to lie above the last place he'd seen Ellison when he'd glanced over the edge.

Ellison was below him. Again Ellison aimed at him, but this time he didn't fire and so figuring his rapid movement had worried his opponent, Dalton stayed still and listened.

He couldn't work out what Ellison would do next, but he figured the gathering darkness was the more important development. He had only to stay free for a short while before he could hide in the shadows.

The first star was breaking through the darkening sky when he heard scrambling, but he struggled to work out where the noise was coming from. Then with a shocked gulp he worked out that someone was behind him.

He turned as Victor bobbed his head up above the other end of the boulder. They considered each other before Victor dropped down from view.

Earlier, when Dalton had climbed up he had found only one suitable route to the top, but a more mobile man could climb up in numerous places. So he trained his gun from side to side as he waited for Victor to show, but when a minute passed without him appearing Dalton felt vulnerable.

He broke off to look over the side; as he'd feared, Ellison had moved on. Dalton presumed he'd also scale the boulder, perhaps coming at him from a different angle and so he didn't wait for them to combine forces and seize the initiative.

With his right leg thrust out while keeping low he skirted around the edge to a spot where the peak of a second boulder abutted against the one he was leaning on. He hoped this would give him one direction from which he could be sure neither man would approach him unseen.

Sure enough, the side of the second boulder turned out to be too precipitous to climb. And between the boulders there was a drop of twenty-five feet that started with a gap of a few feet and narrowed down to a few inches.

As nobody could slip into the gap without him hearing them, he put his back to the abutting boulder. He looked straight ahead ensuring that no matter where Ellison and Victor appeared, he would see them before they saw him.

Five minutes passed in silence with Dalton sitting calmly as he figured time was his ally. If he had to, he was prepared to wait until nightfall for the gunmen to act.

His opponents weren't so patient, but they were organized as, when they came up, they did so simultaneously, appearing at either corner of the boulder, facing him. Keeping their heads lowered, they slapped their gun hands down on rock and picked out his position with uncanny accuracy.

Dalton was already facing to the left and so he aimed at Victor, but before he could fire two gun-shots ripped out. Both shots tore into the rock several yards before him and sliced out a furrow before slamming into the rock at his back.

Dalton kept his cool and fired, but Victor dropped from view and his shot whistled through the air. He moved his arm lower and to the side as he expected him to emerge in a different position, but only a moment later they both bobbed back up again.

This time they had him in their sights and their two shots hammered home only inches from his right boot before they ducked down. Dalton reck-oned that before they re-appeared, he needed to move.

With his legs thrust out before him he shuffled to the side. He had moved for several feet without seeing his opponents again when his trailing hand landed on air.

He fell sideways with a jolt, finding to his shock that in the descending darkness he was nearer to the gap than he'd thought he'd been. Using a frantic flailing motion, he sought to right himself, and luckily that let his gun hand land on the edge of the boulder.

Constrained by his stiff leg, he couldn't twist his body and he toppled awkwardly to the right. He landed on his side with his lower body up to his stomach lying on rock and his upper body projecting out over the gap.

Behind him he heard shuffling, making him tense up, which had the unfortunate effect of making him slip. Slowly at first and then speeding up, he slipped inexorably on, travelling downwards headfirst.

With the narrowing gap in the rock below beckoning him forward, he carried out the only action open to him to still his motion and raised his arm to the other side of the gap.

His right palm slapped flat against the rock, but as he was still holding his gun, he didn't gain enough traction to still his fall and he continued sliding downwards.

He grabbed for the rock with his left hand. Thankfully, this hand found purchase on a projection, stopping him with his body angled downwards and with his legs below the knees pointing stiffly up into the air above the edge.

He reckoned that whichever way he moved, he'd unbalance himself. Then he heard movement as Ellison and Victor raised themselves, so he bent his left leg and placed the sole of his boot against the rockface.

As he'd feared, he didn't find traction and he toppled. In desperation, he tightened his grip around the projection while pressing his other hand to the opposite rock face, and so he pivoted round with his legs scraping against rock.

When he came to rest, he was upright with his legs dangling beneath him and his arms splayed across the gap. He looked up, seeing he was only four feet below the edge, but he'd been lucky in swinging beneath the abutting boulder.

Quickly he pressed his legs to either side of the gap. Then he holstered his gun and edged his hands forward.

Three shuffling movements moved him into the shadows beneath the covering boulder. He was pleased he'd acted quickly as footfalls sounded above him as Ellison and Victor approached the edge.

He stopped moving and looked up, finding that the projecting boulder blocked his view of the top and he could work out where the men were only by their shuffling movements.

'I thought,' Victor said, 'I saw him go over the side.'

'I didn't see him at all,' Ellison said. 'But I reckon he's fled.'

Both men muttered oaths. Ellison's rapid footfalls moved by him and receded.

Victor peered down into the gap, but clearly it was too dark for him to see Dalton as he joined Ellison in hurrying away.

All was silent for two minutes and then Dalton heard scrambling as they clambered down to ground level before starting to talk below him.

Dalton relaxed, accepting he'd evaded being found for now, before he turned his thoughts to how he'd extricate himself from the gap.

Above him the rock was smooth and so his only

choice was to backtrack along the route he'd taken to get here. With his injured leg constraining his movements, he didn't reckon he could turn safely and so he dragged his right hand backwards, feeling along the projection.

He moved his hand for as far as he was able and repeated the motion with his other hand, but the projection that was supporting his weight broke off.

He fell, albeit slowly, but he couldn't find anything to support his weight and so he pressed his forearms and thighs to either side of the gap to control his descent. He held his right leg high to protect it and he was glad he had as his left foot stilled his motion with a jarring thud.

On either side rock was now only inches from his face, while the top of the boulder was ten feet above him. Worse, he'd only stopped moving downwards because his left ankle was jammed firmly in the narrow gap.

When he looked around, his last sight before the light became too dim to see was that the gap only became narrower further down.

CHAPTER 6

Sun-up brought Dalton no respite from his ordeal.

The previous night Ellison and Victor had searched around the boulders until full darkness had descended. Dalton had stayed quiet and they'd not worked out where he'd gone, but by the time he'd been sure they'd moved on, it had been too dark to see his hand when he'd waved it before his face.

Worse, moving for even a few inches was beyond his abilities. His ankle was trapped and the rock to either side was too smooth for him to drag himself upwards.

The only way he could shove himself higher was to put weight on his right leg, but it wasn't strong enough to move him. So he'd found a position in which he could support himself with his elbows and hips while keeping his weight off his trapped ankle.

He'd managed to conserve his strength and so devoted his energies to trying to still his mounting panic through a sleepless night. Now he had enough light to see, he tried moving again, but morning dew had slicked the rock and, when he wriggled, the only motion he made was a few inches downwards.

After that failure, he waited patiently until the rocks were dry while consoling himself with the thought that as he'd slipped downwards, he was still capable of moving. Firstly, he rocked his trapped foot back and forth.

After slipping down earlier, he could now move his foot, but for only an inch in either direction. This was enough to give him hope and so he exerted more pressure.

With his foot arched forward, he was able to strain against the constriction. He pressed for several minutes until, in a shower of crumbling rock, his foot jerked free, making him sigh with relief.

Ahead at his level, the boulders became closer until the gap narrowed to a crack. So while he still had enough strength to move, he decided to shuffle backwards where the boulders spread further apart.

He turned round while supporting as much of his weight as he could with his arms, so that he wouldn't slip downwards again and become trapped. Then he picked his footholds carefully, testing them with the outstretched toe of his boot before he put weight on them.

Over the next thirty minutes, he managed four short steps forward. This moved him for only a yard after which he had to rest his arms, but despite the slow advancement, his success cheered him as he was making progress.

After another thirty minutes of steady movement, he saw that ahead the boulders became further apart until ten yards on the ground became visible.

He moved on, becoming more confident with each step until with a growing desperate urge to extricate himself, he stopped being cautious and scrambled forward. He didn't let his feet rest for more than a few seconds and in the next minute he moved further than he'd managed since the night before.

With each step he dropped down, but that only encouraged him as he was getting closer to the ground. Then his frantic progress provided the inevitable result when he rested his weight on a bump in the rock and it sheared off.

He dropped down and his injured leg wasn't strong enough to stop him, but thankfully his forward momentum kept him moving on. So he went scrabbling down the gap with his hips pressed against the narrowest section and his hands and elbows digging into the rock as he sought to still himself.

Unable to stop his motion, he slid down to ground level where he bent his right leg to avoid jarring it, but that made him land awkwardly and he pitched forward. Constrained on both sides, he couldn't protect himself and his head knocked against the rocky side before he landed on his chest.

He lay, enjoying the feel of the dirt beneath his body after spending so long suspended only a few yards above it while feeling foolish for having hurt himself when he'd been so close to the ground. He dragged a hand out from under his chest and fingered his forehead.

Although he felt only a sore spot, when he got to his knees he felt disorientated. That didn't stop him standing up and, eager now to leave his rocky prison, he made his way along the bottom of the gap.

He emerged in sunlight forcing him to place an arm before his face. The light still made him dizzy and he stumbled before falling to his knees and tipping over on to his side where, with his face shielded, he took deep, calming breaths.

By degrees the pounding in his head receded and he would have gladly lain there for a while, but having survived his perilous situation, the fact he hadn't eaten or drunk for nearly a day gnawed at his stomach.

He looked up at the ridge. Nobody was there, but the sight reminded him that before he put his mind to his own welfare, he had a sad duty to perform.

He stood up and, with a heavy heart and an even heavier tread, he trudged back to the base of the ridge where he looked for Sera's body. She wasn't lying where Remington had found her and so he looked further afield, seeing that her body was now lying beside the boulder where he had taken cover yesterday.

He headed to the boulder while noting the shallow ruts in the ground where she'd been dragged along. The fact that the gunmen, presumably, had moved her but hadn't buried her added to the list of crimes for which they would pay.

She was lying on her chest and so he sat down beside her and murmured a quiet prayer before he turned her over. He judged she was around eighteen, although it was hard to tell as, like her mother, she was lanky; the blood on her face had dried to a thick crust.

Strangely, her eyes were still open and so he moved to close them, but then she exhaled her breath.

He flinched before he got over his shock by telling himself the noise must have come purely from him turning over her body. Then her eyes moved and he couldn't help but speak.

'You're alive?' he murmured.

She didn't reply and so he repeated his question before he leaned over her. With his ear placed above her mouth, he held his breath and he heard and felt her exhale with a gentle wheeze.

He rocked back to give her more air while recalling what he'd seen yesterday. The gunman had shot her, but she'd been moving away from her attacker. Then he'd shot the gunman, who had bled copiously.

This meant she might have avoided serious injury, after all, and the blood that coated her face might not be all her own. As Remington hadn't known this, deeming her to be dead was an easy mistake for him to have made.

Even better, she might have dragged herself to this place.

He located a kerchief and dabbed her cheek. When he'd removed some of the dried blood, his ministrations made her stir and her eyes followed his hand, although they didn't keep up with the movements.

She appeared calm until he dabbed her forehead, which made her murmur in distress, but that helped him to locate a head wound, which when he examined it wasn't as bad as he'd feared. She had incurred a bloody furrow across the temple that suggested the scraping passage of a bullet.

He judged that if the gun had been angled a fraction of an inch nearer to her head when it had been fired it would have killed her. Even so, the shooting of a gun that close to her head had seriously injured her.

'I'm a friend,' Dalton said with a soothing voice. 'I'll get you to safety. Do you understand?'

Her only reply was to blink rapidly, which confused him until he saw that he'd moved and she was no longer lying in his shadow. He stepped to the side so that her face was shaded again and that made her look at him.

Her lips turned up with a slight smile before she closed her eyes. Dalton reckoned that response was the best he could hope for and so he turned his thoughts to practical matters.

He was a day's ride from Lonetree, a journey that had been across barren terrain without any signs of water, shelter or settlements. Based on how long it'd taken him to secure his horse after the Broughton brothers had accosted him, he judged that the journey would take several days even if he didn't have the girl to look after.

He looked up at the top of ridge, seeking an alternative. He was too close to the slope to see if the wagon was still there, but he figured Judah Sundown would have had no use for it and, even if he'd taken the horses, they'd brought provisions.

'Can you walk?' he asked.

Her only reply was to stir and so Dalton slipped a hand beneath her back and hoisted her up to a standing position. When her feet were planted on the ground, he loosened his grip, but the moment he stopped supporting her, she slumped and so he grabbed her again.

'Perhaps later,' he said.

He rolled his shoulders and, with one arm under her back and the other beneath her legs, he picked her up and clutched her to his chest. He turned to the slope and set off.

He didn't get far.

As he'd feared, the shifting rocks that had caused him to slide down to the bottom of the pass provided no resistance. He managed two upward paces only for the rocks to move and make him slide back down again.

Over the next ten minutes, he tried several times, but the climb would have been difficult even if he'd been alone and fit. He put Sera down and reconsidered.

Away from the ridge the ascent of the pass was less steep, but that would necessitate a journey of miles followed by the same distance back, all without assurance the wagon would still be there. He was working out which route up was closest to the ridge when his gaze alighted on the junction between the slope and the pass wall.

Here, larger rocks had congregated. Feeling more hopeful he picked up Sera, this time gathering a grateful murmur that suggested she was aware of what he was trying to do, and set off for the wall.

When he faced the slope, the daunting height he would have to ascend made him pause. So he tore his gaze away from the top and concentrated on planning the first dozen steps up.

He located a flat and sloping rock, which provided him with an easy start. Even better, in crossing the rock he moved into the cooler shadow cast by the ridge and so heartened, he jumped to another flat rock.

For the next fifteen minutes, he made more progress than he'd expected. He had covered a quarter of the route to the top before he had to put Sera down to rest his arms and to stretch his injured leg.

He lay beside her taking deep breaths while

avoiding looking up and depressing himself with the enormity of the remaining task.

From his more elevated position, he could see down the pass letting him imagine the arduous journey back to Lonetree if he failed to reach the wagon. This sight forced him to accept he had no choice but to press on.

'How do you feel now?' he asked without much hope of an answer.

She murmured under her breath and, even when he placed an ear over her mouth and asked her to repeat it, he couldn't work out what she was trying to say. He decided to take her responses as positive signs and picked her up again.

As before, he concentrated on the slope he would have to traverse next rather than planning the whole route up. So in short bursts he moved from large rock to large rock, all the time gaining height.

He didn't reckon his luck would hold out for long and, as it turned out, the rocks soon became smaller. Before long he moved between rocks with a single stride, which made his injured leg ache, and so he sat down against the pass wall with Sera propped up beside him.

'Nearly there,' he said optimistically. 'You looking forward to the journey to town in the wagon?'

She grunted dubiously under her breath, making Dalton smile, even though he couldn't be sure she was responding with a note of realism.

'All right,' he said, 'it might not be that easy, but hopefully when we reach the top we'll have some luck. If we do, we'll be most of the way back to town by sundown.'

'Sundown,' she mumbled and rested her head on his shoulder.

They sat like this for a while, but before long the rising sun poked out above the ridge making the temperature soar.

Dalton set off with the wall at his side. Thankfully, his injured leg was beside the wall, letting him swing up his good leg and then lean against the wall while he moved his stiffer leg.

To his relief he made steady progress. Close to the wall the rocks were jammed in tightly and only rarely did one shift when he put a foot on it.

His progress moved him back into shadow and when he next rested, he was nearer to the top than the bottom.

Despite his growing optimism, his journeys became shorter, his breaks became longer and the temperature rose with the rising sun that eliminated all shade.

Every time he stopped to flex his sore leg and tired arms, he talked to Sera using a conversational tone as if he expected an answer. Sometimes she replied with a murmur and so he figured his comments soothed her.

What worried him the most was that she licked her cracked lips constantly, confirming he had to get her water soon. When he next set off, he kept walking even when his arms felt as if they were being dragged from their sockets and his weak leg throbbed with an insistent demand for rest.

This determined policy provided the desired reward when the going became easier. He thought he was walking over a firmer stretch of the slope, but when he looked up, the slope ahead became less steep.

With a sigh, he accepted he'd covered the worst part of the climb. He slumped down to the ground, this time in relief, and lay her down in the shade behind a rock.

'We're almost there,' he said. 'We'll be able to rest soon.'

'Sundown,' she murmured.

'Long before then, I hope.'

Her only response was to let her chin flop down on to her chest, forcing Dalton to raise her head. He looked into her eyes, but she was struggling to keep her eyelids raised and that was all the encouragement Dalton needed to pick her up again.

This time he held her tightly against his chest as he embarked on a determined walk up the last length of slope. Slowly the scene of yesterday's disastrous encounter with Judah Sundown appeared and Dalton considered the ridge as he searched for the kidnappers.

He couldn't see them and so when the slope petered out and he stood on flat ground again, he

71

turned to the end of the ridge where he and Remington had left the wagon. He groaned.

The wagon wasn't there.

CHAPTER 7

'Just a little further,' Dalton said. 'Then we can rest.'

'Sundown,' Sera murmured.

They'd had this brief exchange a hundred times and now it had become an encouraging litany to himself to keep going.

After the disappointment of discovering the wagon wasn't where he and Remington had left it, he had found wagon tracks that headed towards Lonetree. He was following these and, although on the way here the day before he hadn't looked for landmarks, he figured he was broadly traversing the same route.

As he couldn't recall passing running water, he trudged on without hope, but at sundown the cooler temperature provided relief. Even better, when the darkness spread, he saw a glow ahead.

He sped up, eager to reach the light while he could still see the terrain and he soon confirmed the light was from a camp-fire. A short while later, the sounds of lively chatter drifted to him and so he placed Sera on the ground to plan his next actions.

'We could have had some luck,' Dalton said.

'Sundown,' she mumbled in distress.

'I had promised we'd be on the wagon by sundown, and we might still be.'

'Sun. . . .' she murmured.

She'd gripped his jacket tightly and so gently he opened her fingers, laid her arm across her chest and moved on. He managed three paces before she started keening.

'I won't ever leave you,' he said, returning to her. He stroked her hand until she quietened and then picked her up. 'But you have to stay quiet.'

She nodded, this being one of the most obvious signs she'd provided so far that she was aware of what he was trying to do. Then she started breathing loudly, as if she'd drifted into an uncomfortable sleep.

So with her condition providing him with a mixture of encouragement that she wasn't beyond help and desperation that he needed to act quickly, he moved on.

When he'd halved the distance to the fire, he saw it had been lit beside a rock formation that provided shelter from the wind. The horses and the wagon were to the side of the rock, confirming he'd found Judah Sundown.

Men were milling around and showing no sign they expected trouble. Even so, Dalton veered away to get behind the rock where he placed Sera on the ground.

As he waited for full darkness, he stretched out with his legs before him. Sera was still breathing deeply as if asleep and so quietly he moved a few feet away from her.

When she didn't display any distress, he moved further away, ensuring he could still hear and see her while being far enough away that he could act decisively when the time was right. That moment came when the light from the fire had become brighter than the dim twilight.

He picked his way around the rock and had yet to see the kidnappers when a low murmuring sounded behind him. For a moment he thought one of the men had found him, but then he realized the noises were coming from Sera.

He hurried back to find her rocking from side to side while reaching out as if searching for him. The moment he grasped her hand she stopped writhing and murmuring.

'I reckon,' he said, 'we should stick together.'

She didn't reply other than to gather a firm hold of his jacket and so they set off, as they had done all day, with him carrying her clutched to his chest. He walked sideways with his back to the rock and he reached his first target of the wagon without mishap.

The kidnappers had left a horse still hitched up as they saw to their own needs first, although he would need some luck to take advantage of their mistake.

He raised her to lie her down in the back and clambered inside where he wasted no time in searching for the food and water Remington had brought. With a sigh of relief he found them lying in the corner, untouched.

He brought the water bottle to Sera's lips, but she turned her head away. So, hoping the sound of running water would encourage her, he supped water until he'd relieved his own thirst before he tried again.

The second time he dabbed her lips and she didn't complain, but other than vaguely licking the moisture, she didn't react. When he poured water into her mouth, she made no effort to swallow and the water dribbled out through her lips.

He rocked back on his haunches, now more concerned than he'd ever been about her condition. He sloshed the water before her face and tried again.

This time she managed a sip and, as if that had triggered an unconscious memory, she wrested the bottle from him and put it to her lips herself.

She gulped down two mouthfuls, but then a spasm shook her body and she dropped the bottle. With her eyes wide and sparkling in the low light, she vomited up the water.

When the spasms had stopped, she lay on her side breathing raggedly making Dalton watch her in horror as if every breath might be her last. But, to his relief, her breathing calmed and she felt around for the bottle.

76

Dalton placed the bottle in her hands, but this time he kept one hand on it so he could ensure she only sipped the water and, after two small mouthfuls, he lowered the bottle. She lay on her back and her breathing stayed calm with no sign she'd again react adversely to the water.

'Sundown,' she whispered.

Dalton couldn't work out if she'd fixated on this word because it was one of the first things she'd heard him say or because she was recalling who had kidnapped her. But he decided it didn't matter as she'd spoken more strongly than before.

'You make a better Sundown Kid,' he said, patting her arm, 'than the Sundown Kid does.'

She nodded and so Dalton had just started to calm down when footfalls sounded outside. Then Ellison, one of the gunmen who had followed him down the ridge, spoke up.

'I'm sure the noises came from over here,' he said.

'They did,' Victor, the other gunman, said, 'but they sounded like an animal to me.'

A brief muttered conversation took place and so Dalton held his breath to remain as silent as possible. It worked as two disinterested grunts sounded and the men moved away, but then Judah Sundown's loud and clear voice sounded.

'The noises came from near the wagon,' he ordered. 'Find out what they were before you warm your butts by the fire again.'

Grumbling sounded as the two men returned to

the wagon. A thorough search would reveal them and so moving as quietly as possible, Dalton lay down at the back with Sera.

She didn't appear to be aware of the approaching danger and she gestured vaguely, presumably asking for more water. Dalton placed a comforting hand on her shoulder, but she gestured more frantically and murmured, making the shuffling footfalls outside stomp to a halt, so he put a hand over her mouth.

She uttered a low screech of distress from deep in her throat. Dalton pressed his hand down more firmly, which silenced her, but when it made her struggle Dalton winced in annoyance at himself for making the wrong person suffer.

Anger at the way Judah had treated her welled up in his chest, which, as he was breathing shallowly, made him feel as if he was about to choke. Then Judah shouted an order to Ellison and Victor, the sound of his voice making Dalton snarl.

He removed his hand from Sera's mouth and patted her shoulder. Then he drew his gun.

Figuring that if he planned his next move, it would only prove that fighting back against so many men was foolish, he got up on his haunches and vaulted over the backboard, ensuring he landed on his good leg.

Ellison and Victor were coming around the corner of the wagon and his unannounced arrival made them stare at him in surprise.

Before they got their wits about them, Dalton

blasted two quick gunshots. The first shot caught Ellison low in the stomach making him stumble into the wagon where he hung on to the backboard.

The second shot tore into Victor's neck, downing him. So with time to aim carefully Dalton slammed a second shot into Ellison's side that made him slide away from the wagon before he flopped down over Victor's body.

As consternation erupted around the camp-fire, Dalton accepted that to save Sera's life he had to leave her temporarily, even if that distressed her. He moved on and while seeking the protection of the undergrowth, he reloaded.

The scrub was thickest beside the rocks and when he hunkered down amidst decent cover, Judah was directing the kidnappers to spread out into the darkness. The men responded with frantic haste making it clear they were unsure of the nature of the attack.

Dalton added to the confusion by splaying gunfire across the fleeing kidnappers.

With everyone moving quickly, he caught only one man with a glancing shot to the side that made him stumble before he moved out of sight. Then Dalton looked for a route up the rock.

He located a section that started with a knee-high boulder that he was able to mount before moving across a higher boulder. After clambering over several smaller, flatter boulders, he reached a high rock that even with two strong legs he would struggle to climb and so he made his stand there.

He dropped down on to his chest and wormed his way towards the light finding that he was fifteen feet off the ground and looking down at the wagon. He hoped his absence hadn't upset Sera, but he could do nothing about it as forms were moving in the night.

He couldn't get a clear sighting of any of them and so he stilled his fire. In hushed and urgent tones orders were delivered in the darkness.

Dalton couldn't hear the words, but the concerned tone showed confusion as to the numbers that had attacked them and, confirming his theory, one man ran towards the fire. He kicked dirt over it, extinguishing most of the flames, before running for the horses, where he mounted the nearest steed and moved on.

Dalton let him flee, figuring that if he invited a gunfight, he'd be overcome. Accordingly, two more men appeared from the gloom and they gained horses before galloping away.

The next two men to flee tried to reach the wagon and so Dalton retaliated with rapid shots that made the first man retreat for the horses instead. But the second man went to one knee and, using the light from the spluttering fire, he picked out Dalton's position.

He fired, his gunshot pinging into the rock above Dalton's head. Before the man could get him in his sights, Dalton fired, catching his opponent high in the chest and making him rock backward before he toppled over into the wagon wheel.

Several men appeared together from the under-growth, but the sight of the shot man appeared to convince them they faced superior numbers and they retreated to the horses. Dalton let them go, saving his gunfire until he saw Judah Sundown scurrying towards a horse.

He couldn't let Judah flee unchallenged and he took aim at him before firing, but the light was poor and the undergrowth blocked his sight so he couldn't see if he had hit his target. Long moments passed in which he failed to see him again, giving him hope that he'd been lucky.

Then he saw Judah again, but he'd mounted up and was riding away. Dalton took a speculative shot at his back, but that didn't slow him before he disappeared into the gloom.

Dalton crawled to the side where he noted that only five horses remained. Having shot three men, it was likely that almost everyone had fled, so he wasted no time in climbing down to ground level where, doubled over, he ran for the wagon.

He reached over the backboard and shook Sera's shoulder, the urgency of the situation not allowing him to alert her gently.

'We're leaving now,' he said. 'Everything will be fine.'

'Sundown,' she murmured and briefly clutched his hand. Then he hurried round to the front and clambered on to the seat.

All his activity of the last few hours had stiffened his sore leg making it feel tight and wooden, and so he struggled to raise himself. He gathered a firmer grip of the seat and tugged, but that failed to move him and it was only when he looked down that he understood his problem.

The man he had shot from up on the rock was still alive and he had used the wheel to drag himself upright and grab his ankle.

Dalton tried to kick out, but he couldn't gain enough traction to force his weak leg backwards and so he grabbed the reins instead. A quick tug encouraged the horse to move and a moment later a pained screech sounded that cut off as the wheel rolled.

The man's grip loosened followed by a bump as the wheel rolled over him, and this movement lifted Dalton into the seat. To his right, the kidnappers shouted as they regrouped, but, with his stiff leg thrust out to the side, he trundled the wagon off into the night.

He moved slowly, not wishing to alert the kidnappers and so it took several minutes before the horse reached a fast trot. Then he looked into the back to check on Sera.

The light was too poor for him to see her, but he heard movement; Sera was more animated than he'd expected her to be. She was moving objects around while shuffling towards him.

'Rest,' he called. 'Everything will be fine now.'

He didn't get a reply, but the movement stopped.

As this was an acceptable response, he turned back to the front.

The wagon had trundled along for another minute when a creak sounded behind him, alerting him to a problem a moment before an arm wrapped around his neck from behind and drew him backward. With Dalton being held firmly, someone yanked his gun from its holster and tossed it into the wagon.

'It won't be fine,' Judah Sundown muttered in his ear. 'Your problems have just started.'

CHAPTER 8

'How did you get back there?' Dalton asked when he'd followed Judah's instructions by stopping the wagon.

'I doubled back and rode up to your wagon from behind,' Judah said in his ear. 'Now, where's Remington?'

'He's hiding in the dark watching you. He'll—'

Dalton broke off when Judah yanked him backwards, cutting off his windpipe and tilting his head back over the seat. Dalton fought for balance, but only when Judah loosened his grip was he able to sit back down on the seat.

'I'm no fool. Tell me what you and Remington were trying to do on the ridge. Then I'll end this.'

Dalton raised his chin with defiance. 'If you weren't a fool, you'd have the ransom money.'

Judah snorted. 'If you weren't a fool, you wouldn't have double-crossed me.'

The cold metal of a gun barrel pressed against

Dalton's neck. Dalton strained to move away from it, but Judah had a tight grip around his neck and he'd braced himself against the seat.

No matter which way Dalton turned, he could move for only a few inches before Judah dragged him back.

'Spare the girl,' Dalton said when it became clear Judah wouldn't shoot him immediately.

'Shooting her would be kinder than letting her see your fate.' Judah jabbed the gun into his neck. 'You killed trusted friends and my men are eager to make you regret that.'

With this last comment Judah raised his voice and riders came into view on either side of the wagon. The men all glared at Dalton with surly grins and their hands close to their holsters.

'Do what you will with me, but promise me you'll get Sera back to Lonetree quickly.' Dalton heard Judah snort under his breath and so he persisted. 'It's the only way you'll get the ransom money.'

Judah leaned over Dalton's shoulder while keeping the gun held firm. He laughed before looking at his men, some of whom caught on to his mood and provided supportive laughter.

'I knew you'd bargain for your life.' Judah pressed down with the gun, forcing Dalton to hunch over until he was looking at his knees. 'So make your offer a good one and in return I'll make this fast.'

'Two men stole the ransom on the way to High Pass,' Dalton said using as calm a tone as he could manage. 'Remington and I had to meet your deadline, so we came to the ridge and tried to explain what had happened, but you wouldn't listen.'

'I believe you.' Judah relaxed his gun hand, letting a surprised Dalton sit up straight. 'But I'll stop believing you if you claim you can take me to them, so just give me their names and I'll deal with them.'

'First, we take Sera to Lonetree. Then, I give you their names.'

'That's an interesting offer, but it's not interesting enough. Edwidge Star knew about Marietta's money and he often shot his mouth off when he was with those no-account varmints Lawrence and Hamilton. I reckon they took the ransom.' Judah chuckled. 'Am I right?'

Dalton didn't trust himself to lie convincingly, but he reckoned his silence and tenseness provided the answer. He braced his back against the seat and flexed his legs as he prepared to make a last attempt to free himself.

Long moments passed in which Judah did nothing other than breathe deeply. Then Judah tensed before he edged the gun away from Dalton's neck.

'I want them as badly as you do,' Dalton said encouragingly.

'And in return for your help,' Judah said, his voice uncertain, 'you want me to take the poor, defenceless, sweet young lady back to the loving arms of her mother in Lonetree, do you?'

'That's the deal.'

'Then tell her you've agreed to it.'

Judah removed his arm from around Dalton's neck and so Dalton turned quickly before Judah changed his mind, which let him see that Judah would honour their deal, as he'd had his mind changed for him.

Sera had made a miraculous recovery. She had found Dalton's gun and turned the tables on him by jabbing it into his back.

This was the most controlled action she'd carried out since Dalton had rescued her, but luckily Judah couldn't see the miracle wasn't as unlikely as it'd first seemed. Sweat beaded her forehead and her eyes were manic as she used all her control just to stay upright.

Before her strength gave out, Dalton seized Judah's gun and clambered into the wagon. He claimed his own gun back from Sera, who closed her eyes before she slumped back on to her haunches and then on to her side.

Dalton squeezed by Judah and helped her lie on her back as best as he was able while holding two guns. Then he turned to Judah, who considered Sera's weak state with irritation now he could see she probably wouldn't have stayed conscious for long enough to kill him.

'Tell your men,' Dalton said, 'who's in charge now.'

'I'll tell them who's in charge, for now.' Judah shrugged his jacket as he gathered his composure.

'You can't stay awake all the way back to Lonetree and your young helper can't keep her eyes open until I've finished this threat.'

The latter was true, but Dalton provided a confident smile.

'We'll test your theory and when you're proved wrong, I'll hand you over to the law in Lonetree.'

Judah rocked back his head to laugh with mocking confidence.

'That don't concern me none. Virgil Greeley will release me before sundown and then I'll be free to—'

'Quit with the threats. Marshal Greeley promised to kill you on sight if you ever returned to Lonetree.' Dalton waited for this threat to register, but Judah provided only an unconcerned shrug and so he pointed ahead. 'Now get this wagon rolling back to town.'

With a smile, Judah slipped on to the seat. As soon as he'd shouted instructions to his men to comply with Dalton's wishes, his mocking tone showing he expected nothing of the sort. Dalton sat beside Sera.

'Obliged,' he whispered. 'And this time I mean it when I say you'll be home by the next sundown.'

'Sundown,' she murmured before she provided a wan smile, which was a good enough response for Dalton and he settled down to watch Judah's back while looking out for his inevitable deception.

When Judah moved the wagon on, Sera whimpered restlessly, but she didn't open her eyes and so he let her sleep. He placed her at the back of the wagon where he could check on her condition from the corner of his eye while watching Judah.

Despite his misgivings, as it turned out, they rode on without incident.

Dalton's order that Judah should keep the wagon moving through the night subdued him. So Dalton stayed out of Judah's line of sight, which let him doze for a few moments on numerous occasions so that by first light he felt relatively fresh.

When he peered over Judah's shoulder at the route ahead he felt even more confident as he recognized the high point they were traversing as being the area where the Broughton brothers had stolen the ransom.

Later, Sera awoke and accepted water, but she averted her face from food. Dalton consoled himself with the thought that her condition hadn't worsened since he'd found her, and he settled down with her head resting on his chest and his gun aimed at Judah's back.

Dalton reckoned Judah would act soon, but when they reached Black Creek and moved upriver over land with which he was familiar, he started believing Judah hadn't lied and that he wasn't worried about returning to Lonetree.

Even so, the closer they got to town, the tighter he gripped his gun.

The only sign that Judah wasn't as confident as he claimed was that only half the men who had left the campsite were still with them, the rest having melted into the night. This didn't worry Dalton as Judah was the leader and he'd settle for seeing him delivered to justice.

It was early afternoon and persistent drizzle was starting up when Dalton first saw Lonetree. Judah's only reaction was to glance into the back and smile, before he carried on into town where, without Dalton asking, he drew up outside the Culver Hotel.

Since the previous night, Dalton had been calm about Sera's condition, but with help only minutes away, he couldn't bear to waste even another moment. He kicked down the backboard and clambered out.

He hurried around the wagon and paused to shoot a warning glare at Judah, who returned a mocking salute, before he hurried into the hotel doorway, shouting for Marietta.

Patrons in the hall took up his call and within moments, a flustered-looking Marietta arrived from a back room where she took one look at Dalton before running towards him.

Dalton turned on his heel and by the time Marietta joined him, he was standing at the back of the wagon.

'You have her?' Marietta said, searching his eyes.

'She's been hurt,' Dalton said with a hopeful smile, 'but I reckon she'll be fine.'

Marietta took a deep breath before looking into the wagon at Sera, who was lying beneath a blanket with another blanket cushioning her head. She was lying at an angle that exposed her head wound and Dalton had become so used to seeing it he hadn't considered how shocking it would appear to anyone else.

Marietta screeched in anguish and the sound made Sera flop her head to the side towards her, although as usual she didn't look directly at the person who had made the noise.

The next ten minutes was a distressing time for everyone as Doctor Thornburgh and Marshal Greeley were called. While Thornburgh and Marietta were in the wagon, Dalton explained the situation to Greeley.

He started from the moment Remington had resigned, which proved to be a bad idea as the marshal scowled and he didn't remove the expression even when Dalton had finished.

'I said giving in to Judah Sundown's demands was wrong,' Greeley said, glaring up at the relaxed Judah. 'But I doubt Remington will have the guts to face me and admit that.'

'He did his best in a difficult situation and the Sundown Kid was intent on violence.'

Greeley shrugged. 'Judah is my responsibility now. You'll do nothing more, and that includes dealing with the Broughton brothers.'

Greeley gave Dalton a long look before he turned his attention to Judah, who contented himself with a smug wink before he got down off the wagon.

'You know when we'll meet again,' Judah said to

Dalton before he moved off down the main drag with the remaining four men flanking him and Greeley following on behind.

By the time they'd disappeared from view, Thornburgh emerged to confirm Sera should be taken to Marietta's quarters in the hotel.

He organized two men to bring a board as a makeshift stretcher, but the moment they tried to move her, Sera whimpered and started shaking. Dalton stepped in and, as he had done through most of yesterday, he picked her up and carried her to the hotel.

Sera quietened and, when Dalton caught Marietta's eye, she was smiling for the first time since he'd returned.

He walked along an aisle created through the watching patrons, who burst into spontaneous applause when they saw that Sera was stirring. Thornburgh and Marietta followed on behind and, once Dalton had placed her on a bed, he backed away.

Sera lapsed into unconsciousness again and so he left to give her space. He sat on a chair in the corridor, although he left the door open in case she panicked about him not being there, and a short while later Marietta joined him.

She was biting her bottom lip and she closed the door carefully behind her.

'She went to sleep the moment she lay on the bed,' Marietta said. 'Doctor Thornburgh says that's a good thing and she needs plenty of rest.'

'I'm relieved,' Dalton said. 'For the last day I've been unsure whether she'd live or die.'

'It looks as if it'll be the latter and that's down to you.'

'Not just me. She's a brave young lady to have coped with what happened and to have fought so hard to survive.' Dalton didn't think Marietta would appreciate hearing how Sera had held a gun on Judah and so he limited himself to a simple explanation. 'She saved my life as much as I saved hers.'

'I already knew she'd make a fine woman and if she can cope with all that's happened to her at fourteen, she'll cope with anything.'

Dalton blinked back his surprise. 'I thought she was older.'

'She's tall, like her mother.'

Dalton shrugged before he described events since he and Remington had left town.

The tale of the Broughton brothers' treachery made Marietta wince. When he described Judah Sundown's involvement, she shook her head sadly.

After this revelation, she stared into the middle distance, seemingly paying only cursory interest to the rest of his tale.

'I haven't seen Remington since he left us,' Dalton said, finishing his story with a suitable version of their argument.

'I hope he comes back soon. Believing that Sera died must have been hard on him.' She sighed. 'I promised I'd pay you whatever you wanted if you brought Sera back and I will, but I have plenty to think about with the Sundown Kid being behind this and with Lawrence and Hamilton stealing the ransom.'

'Perhaps when we get the ransom back, you'll be able to pay me.' He waited until she nodded and then slapped a fist into his palm. 'Which gives me yet another reason to find them.'

CHAPTER 9

After the exertions of the previous days, it was several hours after sunup when Dalton awoke, and that was after retiring before sundown.

The rain that had set in the day before had built in ferocity overnight and so the morning presented a dull sight, but it wasn't a depressing one.

When Dalton checked with Marietta, she reported that Sera had enjoyed a restful night. Although she didn't want her daughter to be inundated with visitors and Sera was no longer distressed when Dalton was elsewhere, she let him sit with her.

Sera didn't register his presence, giving Dalton the impression that Marietta was claiming her condition was fine because she was desperate to remain optimistic. Despite this, when Marietta led him aside and asked for his view, he agreed she was making progress.

He asked her if she knew why the Sundown Kid had kidnapped Sera, but she didn't want to talk about him and, after promising to keep Dalton informed of Sera's progress, she left to sit with her daughter.

Despite Greeley's warning to stay away from the Broughton brothers, Dalton wanted to search for the men who had created the crisis. Unfortunately, the intense rain confined him to the hotel.

From the doorway, he watched the few people who ventured out scurry back and forth across the main drag that was rapidly turning to mud while wondering how long he could wait before he checked on Sera's condition again.

As it turned out, Remington Forsyth appeared at the opposite end of town. He was trudging along taking no heed of the pools of water in his path as he was already as wet as Dalton had been when he'd been dunked in the creek.

Dalton expected Remington to go straight to the Culver Hotel, but he veered into the First Star. So Dalton headed outside as fast as he was able.

Despite his speed, when he hurried into the saloon he was drenched and so he sympathized with Remington, who was standing before the pot-bellied stove in a pool of water, clutching a coffee mug to his chest.

'It's a long way back from High Pass afoot,' Dalton said at Remington's shoulder.

Remington swirled round to consider him with surprise. That surprise turned to open-mouthed shock when he saw that Dalton was drier than he was.

'How did you get here first on one good leg?' he said.

'It's a long story and I'll tell you it when you've dried out.'

Remington gave a curt nod. 'I've been dreading breaking the news to Marietta. I assume you've already done that?'

Dalton sat down on a stool and provided a wide smile, preparing Remington for the good news.

'Sera's alive,' he said simply.

Remington flinched, spilling coffee down his chest, although he didn't appear to notice.

'I saw her get shot. Then I found her lying at the bottom of the ridge. She was still and covered in blood.'

'She was unconscious and the blood wasn't all hers. In fact getting shot and nearly being killed was probably the only way she could have—'

'Where is she?'

'She's with Marietta and I'm sure they'll both be pleased to see you, no matter how wet you are.'

Remington closed his eyes for a moment. When he got over his shock, he pointed a stern finger at Dalton.

'If you're lying, I'll punch you all the way back to High Pass.' He slammed his coffee mug on the bar beside Dalton and turned away, but after two paces he stopped. 'If you're not, I'll come back and buy you a drink.'

Dalton didn't reply and, as he was enjoying the

warmth from the stove, he settled down at the bar.

Thirty minutes later, Remington returned. He had changed into dry clothing, but he still appeared tense.

'How is she?' Dalton asked.

Remington ordered two whiskeys before he replied.

'Resting.' He fingered his glass. 'I still don't agree with what you did back in the pass, but I owe you a debt for what you did afterwards out there without no help from anyone.'

Dalton nodded and raised his glass in salute. Then they sat in silence for a while, sipping their drinks.

'Have you spoken with Marshal Greeley yet?' Dalton asked, deciding not to add to Remington's obvious guilt about the situation he'd walked away from in High Pass.

'No, and I have nothing to say to him. . . .'

Remington trailed off and frowned, appearing as if he wanted to say more, but instead he gulped down his whiskey and ordered two more. His pensive expression promised he had a story to tell and Dalton had to decide if he wanted to hear it.

As he doubted he'd ever forget the cold-blooded way Judah had ordered Sera to be killed, Dalton asked the obvious question.

'What's going on here, with the Sundown Kid and Edwidge Star and Marshal Greeley and Marietta and, well, everyone?'

Remington sighed and turned his glass round

several times as he collected his thoughts.

'They've all lived here for years, but as the town grew, all trouble in Lonetree originated from this saloon, so Judah and Greeley dealt with it in their own ways: Greeley used the law and Judah used fear. Last year Edwidge reckoned Judah was becoming too powerful and he ran him out of town.'

'So why did Judah settle his grudge with Edwidge by kidnapping Sera? And how did Edwidge know Marietta had money available?'

'I don't know and we can't ask Edwidge. Apparently, nobody has seen him since we left town.'

Dalton sighed. 'Whatever the reason, I reckon we should make the Broughton brothers explain themselves. They can't get away with stealing the ransom money.'

Remington scowled. 'They'll never return here and I can't expect you to help me search for them.'

'Then think of it this way: I won't get paid for helping Sera until we can reclaim the stolen money.'

Remington snorted a laugh before he pushed his glass away.

'When the rain clears,' he said.

Remington was about to turn away, but their debate had gathered the bartender's interest. He caught Remington's eye, winked, and then pointed upwards.

'Some journeys,' he said, 'are shorter than others.'

Five minutes later, Remington and Dalton were walking along the corridor upstairs to the room the

Broughton brothers had apparently holed up in at first light. They stopped on either side of the door and listened.

Dalton heard nothing within and so he looked at Remington. With gestures alone he agreed their next actions and raised three fingers.

On the count of one, Remington drew his gun. At two, he moved before the door and on three, he kicked open the door.

As Remington charged in, Dalton swung into the doorway. He picked out Lawrence, who was sitting hunched up on the bed while Remington trained his gun on Hamilton, who was nervously tilting back and forth on his chair.

Both men considered Dalton and Remington with wide-eyed concern.

'We didn't part on good terms,' Lawrence said, 'but we didn't expect to face drawn guns.'

'Get on your feet and reach,' Remington said. 'Then you'll explain what you did.'

With nervous gulps and several shifty glances at each other, the two men got up and faced them.

'We didn't steal the ransom money,' Hamilton said quickly, making Remington smile.

'Why would you think we want to ask you about that?' Remington waited for an answer neither man appeared eager to provide. 'And why have you returned to town?'

'Because we live here and because we didn't steal nothing,' Hamilton spluttered with his cheeks red with outrage, although to Dalton this made his attempt to appear innocent look as false as it undoubtedly was. 'You shouldn't listen to Dalton's lies.'

'I don't need to listen to anyone. I saw the empty box you left.'

'We didn't leave no empty box.' Hamilton looked at Remington, who responded with a steel-eyed glare that made him sigh and spread his hands wide apart. When he spoke again, his voice was low and honest sounding. 'We did intend to steal the money, but when we looked in the box it was already empty.'

'How can you expect us to believe that?'

'Because if we'd stolen the money, do you reckon we'd return?'

Remington hunched his shoulders, his gaze appearing uncertain for the first time and when he looked at Dalton, he received a shrug.

'We'll never get to the truth,' Dalton said. 'We have to let Marshal Greeley deal with this. And if he believes them, they'll then only have to convince Judah Sundown they're innocent.'

'The Sundown Kid's back?' Lawrence said, his voice high-pitched with concern.

'He kidnapped Sera.' Dalton smiled. 'And he's got it into his head you two stole the ransom that was meant for him.'

When this revelation made the brothers cast worried glances at each other, Remington holstered his gun. He pointed at each man in turn.

101

'Don't go nowhere and before Greeley arrives, get your story straight and come up with an idea about who did take the money.'

He received stern-jawed looks from both men before he moved through the door. Dalton dallied to deliver warning glares to stay where they were and then followed Remington outside.

'If they didn't steal the money,' he said when they were standing at the top of the stairs, 'that means either someone else stole it from us while we were asleep, or it was stolen before we even left town.'

'We talked with Marietta for only a few minutes before we left,' Remington said before he moved down the stairs. 'On the other hand, we didn't sleep that deeply.'

Dalton nodded. He said nothing more until they reached the boardwalk, where he stopped and considered Remington. Even though Remington's furrowed brow said he couldn't answer his question, he asked it anyhow.

'Clearly the brothers are worried about something, but if the money was stolen while we were in town, who could have. . . ?'

He didn't get to complete his question as a gunshot peeled out. Splinters kicked from the damp boardwalk six inches from his right foot making Dalton go to one knee.

He looked at the buildings opposite, but Remington got his attention and pointed upwards before darting back to the wall.

'The Broughton brothers,' Remington said as another gunshot peeled out from above, 'have given us all the answers we need.'

CHAPTER 10

Dalton followed Remington to the hotel wall while glancing up. Moving quickly saved him from a second shot that clattered into the wood where he'd been kneeling a moment before.

With his back pressed to the wall, the saloon sign above his head blocked Lawrence, who was leaning out of the window, but then Hamilton appeared in the window of a different room. Like Lawrence, he was clutching a six-shooter as he peered at the main drag.

It took him only a moment to work out where they'd gone to ground and he swung his gun down to aim at them. Dalton and Remington didn't waste a moment in taking aim, but that didn't perturb Hamilton and he fired rapidly.

His gunshot sliced into the wall above their heads while their shots clattered into the underside of the sill only inches from Hamilton's hand. Hamilton ignored the distraction and he took careful aim at them.

His calm detachment spooked Remington into darting away from the wall, but Lawrence still fired at him. Remington dodged to the left and right before he found the best direction for self-preservation by ducking and fleeing back into the saloon.

When Hamilton fired again and the shot flicked the brim of Dalton's hat, Dalton reckoned Remington had the right idea.

He ran for the door, reaching it as the batwing swung back towards him. It clipped his shoulder unbalancing him, making his retreat inelegant as well as desperate.

He stumbled for a pace, walked into Remington, and both men grabbed each other to stop themselves falling over. When they'd righted themselves, the customers considered them with bemusement making Remington snarl.

'Since I've returned to town I've wanted to make someone suffer,' Remington muttered. 'It might as well be those two.'

With that, Remington set off for the stairs. Dalton decided to help him by heading to the door.

He gave Remington enough time to reach the first room upstairs before he edged through the batwings. He planned to provide a distraction that would keep Hamilton occupied while Remington burst into his room, but when he looked up, Hamilton was dangling out of the window.

He was hanging on to the sill while looking down as he gathered his confidence to drop. Dalton didn't give him that chance and he stood beneath the sign.

Before he could aim at Hamilton, a shadow flittered on the boardwalk and a scraping sound alerted him to the fact that Hamilton wasn't the only one clambering out of a window. But by then it was too late to stop Lawrence slamming down on his shoulders.

At the last moment Dalton flinched away and so Lawrence's feet caught him only a glancing blow, but even so, his weight sent him reeling into the wall face first.

He rebounded and staggered away for two paces before he went to his knees. He shook his head as he struggled to regain his senses; then he heard splashes.

By the time his vision had stopped swirling, Hamilton had joined Lawrence in dropping down to the street. Both men had fared better than Dalton had done and they were beating a hasty retreat.

Dalton tried to get up, but his attempt failed and he stumbled. He had to put a hand to the wall for balance and, when he drew himself up for a second time, the Broughton brothers had fled to the bottom of Lonetree hill.

He moved gingerly away from the wall, gathering his strength with every pace and, when he'd moved off the boardwalk, Remington was looking at him from an upstairs window.

When Remington saw the brothers had reached their horses, he moved away leaving Dalton to walk on. Dalton sped up as the urgency of the situation forced him to shake off the recent blow.

As fast as he was able, he splashed through the puddles that were now forming into a lake and by the time he'd halved the distance to the bottom of the hill, the mounted men were halfway to the top. Then both men turned in the saddle and raised their guns, forcing him to keep his form small as gunshots sliced into the mud around him.

When Remington joined him, the sheets of rain had taken the gunmen from view. He and Remington wasted no time on discussion before they collected their own horses.

Despite both men's earlier reluctance to head into the torrential rain, within five minutes they were galloping through the puddles after the two men.

After cresting the hill, they were able to get close enough to see their quarries, although they stayed at the limit of their vision. Remington and Dalton didn't try to catch up with them as they headed towards the bridge at Morgan's Gap.

When they approached the bridge, the brothers soon disappeared into the undulating ground and low-lying scrub. Once they'd moved over the bridge, they could either hole up and fight them off, or flee to the north or south, so Remington and Dalton agreed that caution was required.

Slowly they approached the bridge head on, but they saw neither man and so at the water's edge, they stopped to discuss tactics. Remington didn't complain when Dalton offered to cross the bridge first leaving Remington to cover him.

The terrain on the other side of the bridge was of low scrub that provided cover if not protection while the bridge had numerous struts. So while Remington hunkered down behind the right-hand corner stanchion, Dalton dismounted and led his horse down the centre.

He moved as quickly as he could on the slippery wood, ensuring he would be visible between each strut for only brief periods while he looked for movement on the land opposite. He saw nothing other than the swollen Black Creek surging by fifty feet below.

At the halfway point, he reckoned that if their quarries planned to attack him, they should have acted by now. So he peered further afield as he looked for clues as to where they'd fled.

He was thirty feet from land when Remington shouted a warning, making him turn. Then Remington fired rapidly.

The bridge blocked Dalton's view of the land and he couldn't see what had concerned Remington. He hurried to the side of the bridge and peered around a strut at the nearby bank, but he saw no movement there and so he moved to the other side.

He saw nothing untoward, but again Remington fired rapidly making him look at the far bank. He then saw movement as two men went to ground making him wince as he accepted the brothers were one step ahead of him.

They had stayed on the near side of the creek to ambush Remington after they'd split up and when they were at their most vulnerable. He broke into a hobbling run and pounded down the bridge with his gun thrust forward.

The struts on either side of the bridge and the driving rain limited his view of what was happening on land, but the cover also gave him confidence to keep running until he reached the end. He stopped beside the final stanchion where he'd left Remington, but he was no longer there.

He worked out where he'd last seen movement and ducked down before he moved into open space. When he reached a pile of mouldering logs, he knelt and slapped his gun hand on the top of the crumbling wood.

He heard a rustling noise, but it came from some distance ahead. Then Remington shouted and several gunshots rang out, the shots so close together they had to have come from gunfire being exchanged.

From the noise he worked out the shooters were to his right and so he hurried into the damp scrub. Within moments, though, his vision was cut down to a few feet and he had to bat wet leaves and twigs aside to make progress, but he figured everyone would be having the same problem and so he battled on.

He'd covered fifty paces when the scrub thinned out giving him a clear view of the scene. Ten yards away Remington was lying on his chest behind a mound, peering over the top at a rill thirty yards away.

Remington flinched when he heard Dalton fight his way clear of the vegetation. Then he swung his gun round to aim at him, making Dalton stop and raise his hands.

He received a nod before Remington gestured, pointing out the spot in the rill where Lawrence and Hamilton were hiding. Remington directed Dalton to head to a point where he could look down on their quarries while he approached their position from a different direction.

Remington didn't wait for Dalton to agree with his plan. He got to his feet and, with his head down, he ran towards a point forty yards away from where the gunmen were hiding.

Dalton skirted around the edge of the scrub. He had halved the distance to the position Remington had ordered him to claim when, from the corner of his eye, he saw Lawrence bob up briefly over the edge.

Lawrence was ten yards away from the place where Remington had thought he'd gone to ground and the sight made Remington throw himself onto his chest. He landed with a splash in the mud and with his arms thrust out to aim his gun at the rill.

Remington rolled to the side twice, and so when Lawrence rose up again in a co-ordinated move with Hamilton, they blasted lead at his previous location.

Before they could aim at his new position, Dalton hammered a quick shot that sliced into the ground between them, sending up a slew of mud and making both men drop down.

Remington hadn't fired, but when the men disappeared from view, he got up and scrambled on to the edge where he vaulted down.

Dalton reckoned Remington was being reckless, but he could do nothing to help him other than keep moving as quickly as he was able while looking out for the gunmen. He was ten paces from the rill and the other side was becoming visible when more gunfire peeled out.

Lawrence stood up with his gun raised and aimed at the unseen Remington, forcing Dalton to fire. His shot caught Lawrence high in the chest and made him drop.

A moment later two rapid shots rattled. Then Hamilton's raised arms appeared before he dropped with a suddenness that suggested he had been fatally wounded.

Dalton kept running, awkwardly, until he reached the edge at which point he hunkered down. Below, Remington was standing up to his knees in water with his shoulders hunched.

Further along in the water, Lawrence lay face down with only the light current making his arms move while Hamilton lay on his chest with his legs in the water and his face mashed up against the side.

As Dalton clambered down, Remington waded

down the rill and turned Hamilton over. He knelt by him and although Dalton could see Hamilton's lips moving, he checked on Lawrence first.

By the time he'd confirmed Lawrence was dead and he'd joined Remington, Hamilton had stilled.

'Did he explain why they went loco?' Dalton asked.

'Sure,' Remington said with a scowl. 'And it probably explains everything.'

CHAPTER 11

'Who is he?' Dalton asked.

'This is the missing Edwidge Star,' Remington said as he knelt beside the body. 'Hamilton claimed this man stole the ransom, not them, but he wouldn't tell them where he hid it, so they killed him.'

Hamilton had confessed his crimes to Remington before he died and so Remington had led Dalton across the bridge at Morgan's Gap to Edwidge's house. Although the encrusted bloodstains on Edwidge's back said Remington didn't need to check, he turned him over to reveal Hamilton and Lawrence had shot him in the chest and neck.

'The brothers made sure he was dead.' Dalton stood on the other side of the body and glanced around Edwidge's house, noting the open windows and the unsecured door. 'But why didn't they hide his body?'

Remington got up and joined Dalton in looking around. With Dalton taking the right-hand side of the room, they began a systematic search.

'I guess they wanted someone to discover him while they were holed up so their failure to run would make them appear innocent.'

Dalton nodded, but it took another hour before he accepted Hamilton's story. The contents of the house had been strewn around, presumably when the brothers had searched for the money, and so they concentrated their search outside.

Dalton saw that beneath a pile of chopped logs the incessant rain had washed away some of the ground to reveal a sack. Once they'd kicked the logs aside and dragged the sack into the house, Remington wasted no time in opening it up.

He sighed and stood aside to let Dalton see the damp bills, coins and gold that Dalton could imagine amounted to the ransom demand of five thousand dollars.

'So Hamilton was telling the truth,' Dalton said.

'It seems Edwidge stole the money before we left town.' Remington shrugged. 'But I'm thankful we don't have to prove the sequence of events.'

Dalton and Remington directed thin smiles at each other acknowledging they both had no faith Marshal Greeley would be able to confirm the facts either. Then they set about dealing with the situation.

Remington secured the sack while Dalton found a blanket to lay over Edwidge's body, although they left him where he was so the marshal could examine the scene for himself. Then, after securing the door from prying eyes, they left.

When they returned to town, Marshal Greeley was heading into the Culver Hotel, saving them a journey. So, acting nonchalantly to avoid drawing attention to what Remington was carrying, they followed him in.

By the time they reached the corridor outside Sera's room, Marietta and Greeley had finished their brief conversation. So Remington spoke with Marietta while Dalton drew Greeley aside to explain what they'd discovered.

'At last,' Marshal Greeley said with a beaming smile as he showed more animation than Dalton had ever seen from him.

'I thought you'd known Edwidge for years,' Dalton said, unable to hide his surprise.

'Sure, but I never liked him and I never drank in the First Star.'

'But you'll have to prove the Broughton brothers killed him to get their hands on the ransom he stole.'

Greeley shrugged. 'That'll be no trouble. Everyone's talking about the brothers shooting up the First Star and riding out of town with guns blazing. You did the town a service by stopping them.'

Dalton nodded and, lost for a reply, he stepped aside, leaving the marshal to wander off with a skip in his step while whistling a contented tune. He turned away, planning to look in on Sera, but to his surprise Marietta blocked his way while Remington avoided looking at him.

'What's wrong?' Dalton asked as he considered her stern expression. 'I thought you'd be pleased we found the money.'

'I'm grateful for what you did for Sera, but not for finding the ransom,' Marietta snapped. 'That money brings nothing but pain and death to whoever has it.'

Dalton couldn't argue with that and so he stood in silence until Remington gestured at the door, signifying the departed marshal.

'Marietta's told Marshal Greeley she doesn't want Judah Sundown charged,' he said. Remington snorted a harsh laugh. 'He'll be free by sundown.'

'You can't do that,' Dalton blurted out, staring at Marietta. 'For Sera's sake, for your safety, for. . . .'

Dalton waved his arms as he struggled to think of more reasons why she'd made a bad mistake, but she shook her head.

'You'll be leaving now,' she said in a matter of fact manner that sounded like an order.

'I'll leave when the rain stops, which won't be long.'

She bunched her jaw before she went to the sack containing the ransom.

'I told you I'd pay you whatever you asked if you brought my daughter back. You did that. Name your price.'

Dalton shrugged. 'I didn't help your daughter for

the money, but my leg still pains me and so I'd like to rest up somewhere for a few weeks. And I'd like to—'

'Is this enough?' she demanded, dragging a mixture of bills and coins out of the sack without considering how much she was offering.

'That's more than generous.'

She emptied the payment into Dalton's hands and gathered another handful, which she waved in his face.

'In that case, for a man like you, this should be enough for you to leave town now, despite the rain.'

Dalton considered the money and then narrowed his eyes as understanding hit him.

'The Sundown Kid will be free shortly. So you want me to leave beforehand in case he comes looking for me.'

She slapped the rest of the money into his hands, and her haste made bills flutter away and coins tinkle to the floor. Then she spoke slowly and with determination, making her cheeks redden.

'I'm grateful you helped Sera, but I don't care what Judah Sundown does to you. I hate having to deal with men like you and the Broughton brothers and the rest. The sooner you're all out of our lives, the sooner we can return to living decently.'

She flared her eyes, defying him to retort, but as he didn't know why she was angry with him, he reckoned anything he said would only anger her more.

He dropped to his knees. When he'd gathered the money, she was heading into Sera's room, leaving

Remington edging from foot to foot in confusion as to what he should do.

'Go with her,' Dalton said as she closed the door behind her. 'She's upset and once Judah's free, she'll need your help.'

'But how can I help her when I don't understand what's troubling her?'

'I can see you've never been married before, but I have and so the only advice I can offer you is that you'll have to figure that one out for yourself.' Dalton winked, but Remington frowned. 'Whatever her reasoning, she owes me nothing now and either way, I'm not leaving until the rain clears.'

Remington patted his shoulder before he followed Marietta into Sera's room, leaving Dalton to head to his own room.

Despite his comments and although he tried not to, he couldn't avoid pondering why Marietta had become angry with him.

To take his mind off a problem he doubted he'd ever understand, he counted the money. Marietta had been more generous than he'd expected, having paid him over five hundred dollars.

He sat by the window where he wondered how he could use this windfall while watching for signs of the rain stopping. He saw none and although it was hard to tell on such a murky day, darkness was closing in.

He hoped it'd relent by the morning as, with the ransom returned and with the problems he'd been hired to resolve completed, he could move on. But then he saw movement outside.

He peered down the main drag and although he couldn't see the law office, there was activity nearby with several riders having grouped up.

Presently a man walked into view with his shoulders hunched against the rain encouraging the riders to direct a spare horse towards him. The man prepared to mount up, but then he stopped and looked at the Culver Hotel: Judah Sundown had been released.

CHAPTER 12

Despite Dalton's fears about what the night might bring, Judah Sundown didn't return after riding out of town with his men, both those who had been freed and those who had slipped away earlier.

The morning was no brighter, although the rain wasn't as heavy as it had been, giving Dalton the dilemma of whether to leave town or to put his mind at rest first. He figured that even if Marietta was unlikely to explain her anger, he couldn't leave without seeing Sera, no matter how much it annoyed her mother.

He still dallied, reluctant to have another confrontation with her, but when he saw Marietta hurrying across the main drag to the hardware store, he headed downstairs and knocked on Sera's door.

When he heard shuffling within, he glanced around the door. To his surprise, Remington was inside and fussing around Sera's bed.

Remington was clearly deep in thought, as he

didn't register Dalton's presence. When Dalton slipped inside, he flinched and backed away into a chair, toppling it.

'I just wanted to see Sera before I left,' Dalton said.

'I understand,' Remington said quickly, his tone flustered. 'And she's fine, but sleeping, so it'd be best not to disturb her.'

Dalton cocked his head to one side as he considered her, judging she looked healthier than she had the day before, even if she was again asleep. He nodded to Remington and turned to the door, eager now to leave before Marietta returned.

That thought made him realize Remington was probably flustered because he too was hurrying to do something before she returned. He turned back.

'What are you doing?'

'Nothing.' Remington pointed at the door. 'Just go before Marietta gets back and we all have another argument.'

Dalton provided a sympathetic nod and moved to turn away, but then he saw the bag lying beside the bed with clothes poking out of the top.

Remington saw where he was looking and he kicked the bag out of sight before with a shrug he acknowledged he was acting oddly.

That made Dalton note Sera's blankets had been moved aside, while a second door at the end of the room that had always been closed before was now open.

'Are you planning to take her away?'

'I'm . . . I'm taking her somewhere where I can keep her safe. The Sundown Kid will return and I can't assure her safety here.'

'Sundown,' Sera murmured, showing she had yet to shake off this habit.

Dalton narrowed his eyes. 'Marietta doesn't know about this, does she?'

'She doesn't, but then again, she invited him here.' Remington raised a hand when Dalton started to ask one of the many questions on his mind. 'You have to trust me on this.'

'I do trust you.'

'Then let me leave.' Remington shooed him away. 'And keep Marietta talking for as long as possible.'

Remington shot him an imploring look. Dalton was still minded to demand a fuller explanation, but then he heard the main door open forcing him to make a quick decision. He gestured at the other door and turned away.

While Remington bustled, he slipped into the corridor and closed the door behind him. As he expected, Marietta was approaching and she considered him with a harsh glare, but she did at least stop.

Dalton put on the biggest smile he could manage and walked towards her.

'I wanted to look in on Sera before I left,' he said using a placid tone.

'You've done that,' she snapped. 'Now go.'

'I will. I'll head downriver and I doubt I'll ever ride this way again, so you'll probably never see me again, but I hate parting with you . . . with anyone, on bad terms.'

'So do I, but you'll have to accept I can't explain.'

She moved to walk by him and so he side-stepped to block her path.

'Why can't you explain?'

'I've thanked you and I've paid you. I don't owe you nothing now. Move aside.' She glared at him, but Dalton returned an equally resolute look that showed he wouldn't move. She sighed and continued in a more conciliatory tone. 'All right, but I don't want my daughter to overhear. I'll check on her and then we'll talk.'

The nature of her unexpected capitulation gave Dalton no choice but to let her pass. He still did so slowly and then he followed her while wincing in anticipation of the inevitable outcry.

Sure enough, within moments of going into Sera's room Marietta came storming out with her fists clenched and her eyes blazing.

'Perhaps you should explain now,' Dalton said, 'and then I'll explain.'

'I'm telling you nothing. Where did Remington take my daughter?'

'He's keeping her safe. He's worried the Sundown Kid will come here.'

'He will do, but that's only so I can make sure Sera will always be safe. I don't want the money, only my daughter.'

Dalton shrugged. 'I've never heard of anyone

123

paying a ransom demand after the hostage has been freed.'

'They might do if they had no use for the money. We'll be better off without it and either way, none of this is your concern.'

Dalton considered her aggrieved gaze and posture, and then frowned.

'It is when the Sundown Kid is around and he's promised to kill me.'

'Then that's all the more reason why you should leave now.' She flashed a triumphant smile. 'I'll let you guess when he'll be coming here to collect the money.'

Dalton turned away. 'In that case, if I meet Remington, I'll tell him when it'll be safe to bring Sera back.'

'Tell him if he doesn't bring her back immediately, I don't ever want to see him again.'

Dalton headed to the door. 'As you told me, that's not my concern.'

Before she could retort, he slipped outside and stood beneath the boardwalk canopy to ponder on where Remington had gone.

He didn't know the area well enough to make a sensible guess, but when Marshal Greeley came scuttling towards him, he decided braving the rain on a fruitless search was preferable to finding out what the marshal wanted.

With a hobbling gait he hurried off making Greeley shout after him, but he didn't look back. He decided to start gathering information about where Remington might have gone from the well-informed bartender in the First Star, but the moment he went into the saloon he regretted his decision.

The Sundown Kid had taken up residence there.

He, along with the men who had been in High Pass, were splayed out around the saloon room, drinking steadily while casting glares at anyone who came in that were so surly they'd driven most of the customers away.

'I see,' Judah said, 'you've saved me the trouble of coming looking for you.'

'And I'm pleased you're here so I can give you a warning,' Dalton said. 'Everyone knows where you'll be at sundown. Harm nobody or I'll be the one who comes looking for you.'

The eager grins on the faces of Judah's men disappeared and two men scraped back their chairs and stood up, but Judah raised a hand, ordering them to sit down.

'Nobody has forgotten what you did in High Pass, Dalton.'

'And you shouldn't forget you've only just been released from the jailhouse.'

'You reckon I'm worried about Marshal Greeley?'

Dalton tried to reply, but raucous laughter drowned him out. When that petered out, a new voice spoke up from the doorway.

'You should be,' Marshal Greeley said. 'I released you because the charges against you were dropped and because I have no proof about anything else you've ever done in this town.'

Judah turned to face the newcomer. 'You won't do nothing, Greeley. You never had the guts to take me on before and that won't ever change.'

'Except I never wanted to take you on. I kept the peace while you did whatever Edwidge told you to do.'

Judah laughed. 'Not any more he won't after the Broughton brothers filled him with holes.'

'I hated Edwidge, but he was twice the man you or I will ever be.'

'There's only one person who can compare the three of us. Do you want to take back that claim?'

Judah looked around the saloon room. He caught everyone's eye, except for Dalton's, with an obvious encouragement to laugh, and his men took the opportunity.

For his part Greeley stood two paces in from the door with his hands on his hips looking more determined than Dalton had ever seen him, making Dalton wish he knew what they were taunting each other about.

When the laughter died down, Greeley still looked at Judah; silence descended and Judah shuffled uncomfortably on his chair. Then Greeley smiled.

'No,' he said emphatically.

He waited until Judah's right eye twitched before he turned on his heel and walked out of the saloon.

With Dalton seemingly forgotten about, Judah

stood up and followed. When he stopped in the doorway his men moved after him, giving Dalton only a limited view of Greeley picking a route between puddles as he made his way down the main drag.

'Hey, Greeley,' Judah shouted, drawing his gun. 'I've got my answer.'

Greeley jumped over a puddle before he turned to face Judah.

'I'm not interested in anything you—' Greeley trailed off and scrambled for his gun, but before he reached it a gunshot blasted out.

Judah's men snickered as Greeley clutched his chest. Blood seeped through his fingers and dripped into the puddle at his feet, creating a dark patch that swirled and broke up as the rain pattered down.

Greeley fell to his knees in the water before keeling over, face first, into the puddle with a splash that sent the water skating away.

Everyone in the saloon edged forward, but as the water dribbled back to settle around Greeley's body it was clear he wouldn't get back up. It was also clear that with Judah and eight men to face, Dalton couldn't do anything other than get himself killed and so while their attention was on Greeley, he sought a way out.

The bartender saw his problem and beckoned him. So in short order Dalton hurried across the saloon room and slipped over the counter.

The bartender directed Dalton to a back door that

he made for without a backward glance. Then he skirted around the backs of the saloon and the three adjacent buildings.

Only when he reached the corner of the stable on the edge of town did he pause for breath. He figured that after shooting the marshal, Judah had nothing to lose and any deals he'd made with Marietta were as irrelevant as Remington clearly reckoned they were.

It was several hours until sundown and so Dalton reckoned he had time to act. Keeping in the shadows of the buildings, he worked his way back to the main drag.

Greeley was lying where he had fallen and nobody had yet to venture outside, but that also meant Judah was still in the saloon. He hurried on and reached the Culver Hotel without incident.

Marietta was pacing the corridor and looking concerned, and unlike before she relaxed when she saw Dalton had returned.

'Judah shot Marshal Greeley,' Dalton said simply. 'You have to leave town now.'

CHAPTER 13

Thankfully, when Dalton headed over Morgan's Gap and turned downriver, he saw the small wagon they had taken to High Pass standing outside Edwidge's house.

Marietta didn't know where Remington might have gone and this place had been Dalton's only hunch. Before he drew up, Remington appeared at the door, but when he saw Dalton wasn't alone, he slipped back inside.

'I didn't expect you to follow me,' he said when Dalton hurried inside, 'or to bring her here.'

While Dalton frowned, Marietta brushed past him to check on Sera, finding her lying on folded-over blankets by the wall beside the spot where they'd found Edwidge's body. She was sleeping as quietly as usual, at least proving the journey hadn't caused her undue distress.

'I had no choice,' Dalton said. 'You wouldn't have

had a wedding to look forward to if I hadn't let her see her daughter.'

'Wedding or not,' Remington said, 'she's not taking Sera back to Lonetree.'

'I reckon that argument has been won.'

Dalton looked at Marietta, who paused from fussing over her daughter to explain what had happened.

'We have to get as far away as we can,' Remington said when she'd finished. 'Lonetree is no longer safe.'

Remington and Marietta glared at each other with their lips pursed, this clearly being a continuation of their earlier argument that had led to Remington bringing Sera to the cabin.

'As the Sundown Kid wants me dead too,' Dalton said when they'd both been silent for a while, 'can someone explain what's happening?'

'Sundown,' Sera murmured, making Marietta tense.

'All right,' Marietta said with her teeth gritted.

'You've always told me I don't have a right to know,' Remington snapped, 'so why are you going to tell him the truth?'

'His life is in as much danger as ours, so he has a right to know.' Marietta gestured at Dalton. 'Provided he stops referring to Judah by that name.'

Remington nodded. 'And that's why you got annoyed. Sera's hardly spoken and then all she has said is—'

'Sundown,' Dalton said, interrupting as he worked out why Marietta had become angry with him. 'It was the only word she said while I was bringing her back to town and I thought that was accidental, but perhaps it isn't because you don't want her ever using that word.'

Marietta caught both men's eyes and pointed at the door before she headed off. Dalton and Remington followed and outside, Marietta stood on the porch in a position where she could watch Sera, but where the rain pattering on the canopy would drown her voice.

'I don't want her to know that Judah Sundown could be her father,' she said.

Remington raised his hat to brush his fingers through his hair, although his expression didn't change suggesting this explanation wasn't a surprise.

'And is he?' he said after a while.

'Back when I opened the hotel, life wasn't as it is now and people weren't as they are now.' She lowered her head. 'It could be several men.'

'Who else?'

'Judah is the only one who's still alive.'

'Edwidge Star?' He waited until she nodded and slapped his thigh in irritation. 'I knew there was something wrong there.'

'It's worse,' she said, her voice small. 'Marshal Virgil Greeley too.'

Remington winced. 'Any more?'

'Just those,' she declared, her voice becoming

indignant now she'd revealed her secret, 'and as it is between those men, you can see why I'd prefer her to never know anything.'

Remington tipped back his hat. 'One man who tried to kill her, one man who didn't care if she lived or died and a man who never wanted anything to do with her.'

'It's not quite as bad as that.'

Her voice had become quieter until she was eventually silent, but Dalton had heard enough to piece together the final element.

'Edwidge Star didn't know about the others and he cared enough to pay for your silence. He paid you small, regular amounts, but you never spent the money. So after fourteen years, it grew into a tidy sum. Then Edwidge found out you'd never used it.'

She nodded. 'I never wanted it, but I thought it'd ensure Edwidge's silence. So I kept it for Sera for when she grew up. But Edwidge was a gossip and he must have told Judah and the Broughton brothers about the money. Judah kidnapped Sera to get revenge against Edwidge, while Edwidge stole the ransom to stop Judah getting his hands on it.'

With the truth revealed the three of them stood in silence. Marietta looked at Remington for his reaction, but when he said nothing and didn't even look at her, she went back in the house.

'What do you think about that?' Dalton asked Remington.

'I understand why she's fought to keep the truth hidden,' Remington said.

'Perhaps she was right and the Sundown . . . Judah will take the ransom and leave, as clearly that's all he cares about.'

'He won't leave.'

With a sorry shake of his head Remington headed inside where he asked Marietta about Sera's condition. As his light tone sounded like they were starting to reconcile, Dalton left them alone and sat on the porch in a dry spot.

He pondered on Remington's final comment, wondering if Judah would leave after he'd claimed the ransom. Judah probably wouldn't want to run the saloon after Edwidge's demise, but there was a chance he wouldn't find the money she had left at the hotel, which made him wonder if he'd misunderstood Remington.

He considered the wagon. He shook his head, trying to dismiss the wild idea that had occurred to him, but it refused to go away and so he hurried over to it.

He peered in the back and sure enough, the box that had previously contained the ransom was there, the ransom once again intact. Remington had presumably brought it in defiance of Marietta's wishes.

As the light level dropped, this discovery made his assessment of the situation become even gloomier until with a sigh he went inside. Remington and Marietta were sitting together against one wall.

They looked shamefaced with their argument seemingly talked out, which made Dalton recall the times when he too had once enjoyed family life. They were facing Sera and so with a smile, Dalton went over and hunkered down beside her.

Sera was breathing naturally and her colour was strong, so he ran the back of his hand over her cheek, receiving a contented murmur while her eyelids fluttered. He waited and presently she opened her eyes and met his gaze.

Her eyes widened with delight and she smiled, before she closed them again and returned to her previous state.

'It's nice to see how much calmer she is when she knows you're near,' Marietta said.

Dalton nodded, but Remington shook his head.

'A fight's coming our way,' he snapped, seemingly irritated that Sera had enjoyed seeing Dalton. 'We can't sit here kicking our heels.'

'We don't know Judah will come,' Marietta said, 'and even if he does, where can we take her?'

Remington frowned, clearly lost for an answer, but Dalton raised a hand.

'I'll let you work this out,' he said. 'I'll keep lookout.'

When he left, they didn't register his departure as they started discussing options. Outside, Dalton stood on the edge of the porch.

The rain was pelting down on the wagon, sending raindrops bouncing two feet in the air, but the sky was lighter upriver. He judged it was around sundown.

Dalton looked in on the house. He smiled. Then he drew the brim of his hat down low and traipsed into the rain.

Without preamble he gathered up the reins for his horse and Marietta's steed and clambered on to the seat. Working as quietly as he could, he moved the wagon off.

Holding on to two horses while steering a wagon wasn't easy, but to his delight he moved away from the house without anyone appearing.

He presumed the noise of the pounding rain and the discussion inside was keeping them from noticing his departure, so he was two hundred yards away before Remington came out and looked around.

It took him several seconds to notice Dalton after which he did a double take and hurried away from the house. He splashed through the mud and then found out how slick the ground was when he slipped over and went sliding along on his chest.

Dalton's last sight of Remington before the terrain took him out of view was of him kneeling in a puddle and slapping his hat to the muddy ground.

Then Dalton speeded up and headed for the bridge at Morgan's Gap.

When Dalton drew the wagon to a halt on the top of Lonetree Hill, the rain had stopped and Marshal Greeley's body had been taken away.

The townsfolk weren't visible, but the improvement in the weather had encouraged Judah Sundown and his eight men to loiter outside the saloon. For the first time in days the low cloud was lifting from the horizon and the sun was threatening to poke out, showing it'd be sundown within fifteen minutes.

Judah was looking towards the Culver Hotel. Presumably, he expected Marietta to be waiting for him with the money, but knowing that didn't help Dalton.

Seeing the number of men below brought home to him how foolish he'd been to ride off and face them alone. If he were to prevail, he needed a plan beyond just riding into town and confronting Judah.

He had released the horses after he'd gone over the bridge as holding them was slowing him down. So Remington could be here soon and, as he was doing this to protect him, he needed to act quickly.

He thought back through everything that had happened since he'd first come across the wagon, a thought that made him smile as this old, rickety wagon had been involved in most of the prominent incidents that had happened: the Broughton brothers had pushed him into the creek on it; the ransom had gone missing from it and starting everything; he'd brought Sera back to town on it and Remington had taken Sera away on it.

He'd been pushed into the creek on it. . . . That

thought gave him an idea, except this time he could use a runaway wagon to his advantage.

Dalton took the wagon away from the crest of the hill to ensure it would be out of view from below and then crawled back to the edge to consider the lie of the land.

He figured the well-worn trail down the hill would ensure the wagon rolled towards the saloon, and this would attract Judah's interest. When it reached the main drag, Judah would recognize it as being Marietta's and investigate.

Hopefully he would see the box on the back and, guessing what it contained, he would try to reach it, but equally hopefully the wagon would have enough momentum to roll past the saloon. The incline then became steeper and, if Judah didn't get to it first, would ensure the money would plough down into the creek.

This plan had many unknowns and Dalton was unsure how they would play out, but he figured the confusion would let him seize the initiative. As the sun poked out beneath the clouds, he got to work.

He unhitched the wagon, let down the backboard and removed the canopy so the box would be visible from the back, ideally for the first time as it passed the saloon. Then he shoved the wagon towards the edge before moving on to consider what he would do after he released the wagon.

He figured he'd have to act quickly to move the wagon and then mount the horse. Then he'd have to head down the hill unseen to reach a position where he could attack Judah while he was distracted.

Unfortunately, no matter which route he took, he didn't reckon he'd have the time to get into town without being seen even though the light level was dropping as the sun edged towards the horizon. He slapped the wagon in frustration at having wasted time on a plan that probably wouldn't work before he moved to the back and clambered up.

He wondered where he could leave the money while he tried a different plan, but then he saw a rider approaching. He lay down on his front to watch him until he saw that Remington was coming, having clearly located his horse faster than Dalton had anticipated.

Dalton put aside his annoyance and beckoned him on.

'I wanted to avoid this happening,' he called as Remington drew up before the wagon, 'but as it's turned out, I need your help.'

Remington didn't reply as he dismounted and appraised the situation. He glanced at the route to town and nodded.

'I can see what your plan was,' he said, 'but like your plans at High Pass and Morgan's Gap, it's another poor one.'

'I left you at Morgan's Gap for a good reason.'

'I know. You're a brave and resourceful man, while I'm only fit for floundering in the mud.'

'I didn't do it to make you look bad. I once had a

family; you could have what I was denied. I was helping you.'

Remington got up on to the wagon to join Dalton where he kept low to avoid being seen from the town.

'That was your intent, but after you've moved on, how can I be a father to Sera when the only man she's ever looked at with gratitude is you?'

'I can't answer that one now.' Dalton pointed at the red sun. 'We need to act quickly while we still have a chance.'

Still annoyed, Remington slapped his hand away and with Dalton standing in a crouched position, the blow was strong enough to tip him over. He fell against the box and his weak leg gave way sending him sprawling towards the front of the wagon.

'We will,' Remington called as he jumped off the wagon, 'but with Sera's and Marietta's lives at stake, this time you will follow my orders.'

Dalton grunted that he agreed as he moved to follow him, but then he jerked forward.

The movement caught him by surprise and it took him several moments to realize that when he'd fallen heavily, his motion had moved the wagon. He righted himself, but that took some effort as the wheels were still rolling, and when he looked round with concern, he could see down to the town.

Clearly the wagon had crested the top of the hill and it was rolling down the side. He turned back aiming to get off, but already Remington was a dozen yards away and staring at Dalton in horror.

The trundling wheels took Dalton away down the slope. Within moments, the wagon was moving so quickly, he didn't dare jump.

CHAPTER 14

Dalton dropped down on to his chest. Then he squirmed to the front of the wagon where he raised himself to look at the path ahead.

As he expected, the wagon was rolling down the main trail, having slipped into wheel ruts that would ensure it reached the main drag through town.

Where it would go then was still uncertain, although Dalton's bigger concern was whether he'd still be on board when it reached the town.

As had happened upriver, the wagon was shaking so much he couldn't keep his balance and the noise of the rattling wheels made it sound as if the wagon would collapse at any moment. The box was rocking from side to side appearing in danger of being bounced off the back and so Dalton clamped a hand on the lid.

That stopped it moving and it also let him brace himself between the box and the side. He looked up the slope, seeing he'd rolled for a hundred yards and

Remington had moved out of sight.

Dalton hoped Remington would get over his shock quickly and help him, as the wagon was shaking so much he couldn't do anything to help himself. Even though he kept his head down, every obstacle in the wagon's path bucked him up into the air, letting him see the town ahead.

So in intermittent flashes he saw one of Judah's men get his attention. Judah faced the approaching wagon with his hands on his hips. Then he ordered two men to investigate, but they were wary of what danger the runaway wagon might present and they stayed back.

By the time he was halfway down the hill, he was travelling fast enough to reach the saloon within a minute while Judah and his men had formed a line to watch the wagon approach.

His hopes that the arrival would sow confusion in their ranks didn't appear to be materializing. Worse, as the trail became less defined with numerous other routes into town becoming available, the wagon found its own route down the hill.

The wagon bounced over two wheel ruts, knocking Dalton to the front. Then he tumbled backwards over the box to leave him lying sprawled over it with his head mashed against a side and his weak leg lying over it.

When he'd righted himself, the main drag was no longer ahead and the wagon was veering to the left to take a new route towards the saloon. Judah was still watching the wagon without apparent concern, but one of his men yelled something and pointed at it.

Dalton presumed he'd been seen and so he clamped a hand on his holster in preparation of defending himself, provided he survived crashing into the saloon. He felt more optimistic about that possibility when the wagon reached smoother ground and it stopped bouncing around.

Even though he was travelling at a speed that would be nerve racking when being dragged along by horses, he felt more secure than before. So he risked looking forward again.

The saloon was a hundred yards ahead and he was within a dozen wagon lengths of the bottom of the hill. Judah had spread his men out to take up positions to either side of his potential route and Dalton's best guess was he'd slam into the wall beside the right-hand window.

Dalton hugged the base of the wagon, seeking a handhold, but he couldn't find one on the rain-slicked wood. A few moments later a thud heralded he and the box being bucked into the air before a splash sounded as the wagon ploughed into the mud.

Water sprayed up to create curtains of muddy water on both sides of the wagon that were fifteen feet higher than Dalton's head. With every roll of the wheels through the thick mud the wagon slowed, sending Dalton tumbling up against the front board.

Before, when he'd worked out how fast the wagon

would roll through town, he hadn't taken account of how slow the going would be. Now he doubted he'd even reach the saloon, although as he was unable to see through the shower of mud, the only ways to judge his progress were the squelching wheels and his movement in the wagon.

After being thrust up against the front, he slid into a corner, suggesting the wagon was slipping around to slide sideways. Then he suffered a disorientating moment when the wagon tipped to the left before it slopped back down on to its wheels and spun round.

Dalton went careening around the base until, with a lurch, the wagon stopped with him pressed into a corner on his back and with the box tipped up on its edge, lying against his chest. He peered around the side to be faced with the confusing sight of the saloon seemingly standing at an angle.

Then he refocused and accepted the wagon was standing side on to the saloon with two wheels having mounted the boardwalk, leaving him wedged into the lower corner.

'That was lucky,' someone called. 'I thought it'd go rolling into the saloon.'

'Be quiet,' Judah said. 'I'm sure someone was hiding in the back.'

A murmured conversation ensued after which squelching footsteps sounded as two men made their way round the wagon. They both stopped and leaned forward to peer into the back.

Smiles appeared as they saw the box, which rapidly

disappeared when they looked past it at Dalton and his drawn gun. Two quick gunshots tore out.

Dalton's first shot took the nearest gunman through the chest making him drop to his knees before he keeled over to lie face down in the mud. The second shot winged the other gunman making him stumble, but he fought off the pain and drew his gun.

Before he could raise it, Dalton planted a slug in his forehead that cracked his head back, making him topple over backwards.

While consternation broke out behind him, Dalton shoved the box aside and sought the other corner of the wagon so he could be in a different position when the gunmen organized themselves.

With the wagon being at an angle, moving while keeping his head down proved to be harder than he thought it'd be and it took Dalton several moments to slide across the base to the other corner. He ended up in a low sitting position with his back against the side and his legs splayed across the wagon floor and braced beside the box.

He waited with his gun thrust forward for the gunmen to make their next move, but as he'd feared that turned out to be wild gunfire.

They must have lined up facing the wagon as round after round tore into the wood; thankfully most of it was aimed at the spot where he'd been sitting previously.

The wood deflected some of the gunfire, but most

of it burst through. Several shots hammered into the box, saving his lower body, but all he could do to protect his upper body was to make himself as small as possible.

Being pressed tightly against the base and side proved to be the right place to be and Dalton assumed he'd inadvertently lain in a position where the seat protected him, as after reloading twice none of the shots came close.

The gunfire must have looked impressive as loud whoops sounded. Then the wagon lurched as a wheel broke, leading to more whoops.

Judah ordered someone to investigate. Despite the encouragement ringing in his ears from the other men, this man moved more cautiously than the previous two gunmen had.

Slurping footfalls sounded as the man approached the seat. Then he moved round to the side, but he didn't come into view, making Dalton realize he was creeping along, crouched over.

He got confirmation of the newcomer's plan when a hand clutched the opposite side of the wagon before the man raised himself. The moment his forehead came into view Dalton fired.

His shot clipped only wood, but it landed inches away from the man's hand and made him rock away, but with his hand clamped down firmly on the side he pushed down and managed to lower the wagon.

The movement made Dalton slide along the slippery base and his redistributed weight made the wagon tip faster. Then a crack sounded as the broken wheel gave way and the already precariously positioned wagon tipped over on to its side.

Dalton went sliding down to the side where his momentum made him fall out of the wagon and go sprawling in the mud on his knees. Laughter sounded until the man who had sneaked up on the wagon cried out.

'I was right,' he shouted. 'That is the box of money.'

'So kill him,' Judah said, 'and get the box.'

Dalton turned on his knees to face a line of seven men, all with guns drawn and all smirking as they took aim.

With a hopeless feeling in his guts, Dalton swung his gun towards Judah while, almost as a harbinger of his impending doom, darkness overcame him.

The gunmen didn't fire; instead they laughed, and Dalton saw the reason for their behaviour when the darkness became deeper. Then he realized what had happened and he prostrated himself in the mud a moment before the wagon tipped over and slammed down over him.

In the darkness Dalton raised a hand to the base of the wagon, finding it had come to rest two feet above his head. He pushed, but the base didn't move and worse, clattering sounded as Judah and his men clambered on to the top.

A moment before they acted, Dalton anticipated what they'd do. With his good leg he pushed himself to the side, the mud letting him slip along with ease.

His quick reaction saved him from a burst of gunfire that tore down through the base making holes of light burst out above the place where he'd been lying.

This time, Dalton reckoned he could use the same tactic.

The moment the gunfire stopped, he aimed at the spot where the men had fired and blasted off two quick rounds before he rolled to the side.

'Get off the wagon,' Judah shouted.

As Dalton reloaded, stomping sounded from the men moving away. Before they got off, Dalton fired at the position where he'd heard Judah.

He was rewarded with a cry of pain and a clatter-ing sound as someone flopped down on the wagon above his head. A second thud sounded as another man got off the wagon, but then fell heavily against the side.

Someone fired down at the wagon, splaying gunfire wildly, but with Dalton lying beneath the body none of the shots came close. His delight was short-lived as Judah ordered the man to get off the wagon, confirming he hadn't hit the leader.

'He can't keep avoiding us,' someone said.

'He won't,' Judah said. 'End this.'

Silence reigned and unlike before, Dalton heard no hints of what the men were doing.

For his part he used the light shining through the bullet holes to locate the box and shuffled closer to it, although he was unsure where the gunmen would be when they fired at him again.

A creak sounded above, giving Dalton a warning of what they planned before a sliver of light appeared along one side of the wagon. When Dalton realized they were righting the wagon, he shuffled behind the box from where he peered at the expanding gap.

When the gap grew to a foot high, Dalton saw three men standing on dry ground in the centre of the drag, suggesting the other two men were righting the wagon.

He could see only their boots, but he reckoned he could still inflict damage and so he aimed at the right ankle of the central man, figuring that man would be Judah.

Unfortunately, Judah must have been aware of the possibility of this response as the men blasted a round apiece at the gap, forcing Dalton to retreat behind the box. But it also made the men who were tilting the wagon shout out in complaint that they were behind the line of fire.

The wagon thudded back down. Then more gunfire erupted.

Dalton cringed, but none of it hit the wagon and even better, rapid footfalls beat a hasty retreat, making him hope that this showed that Remington had made his way down the hill unseen and was helping him.

For several minutes silence dragged on. Then the gap opened up again, and this time nobody was visible.

Dalton judged they'd try the same tactic as before, except they might learn from their mistakes and fire systematically into the wagon from numerous angles. Before they started, Dalton seized the initiative.

He shoved the box towards the nearest corner. The muddy ground helped him move it quickly and as he'd hoped, the box slipped into the expanding gap as it became wide enough to accept it.

This gap was also wide enough to let Dalton slip through and so he snaked under the back of the wagon with his gun thrust out before him. He could see nobody ahead and so as he emerged, he twisted to the side.

His foresight was rewarded when he found himself looking up at one of the men who were tugging the wheels to tilt the wagon. The man released the wheel and threw his hand to his gun, but not before Dalton planted a slug in his chest that made him fall away.

The other man who was tilting the wagon alerted Judah with a strident cry and, when he released the wheel, the edge of the wagon pressed down on Dalton's back leaving only the box to keep the corner elevated.

With his manoeuvring space reduced, Dalton stayed where he was and looked for the other men. Gunfire sounded and so he hugged the ground, but unlike the previous time he didn't hear shots slice into the wagon.

Then at the far corner of the wagon an agonized cry sounded followed by a heavy clatter that had probably been made when the other man who had stayed with the wagon fell over.

He reckoned Remington had shot this man, but Judah's remaining men were closing in on him and so he needed to get out before they trapped him. He squirmed, but the edge was only inches above the small of his back and he struggled to move over the soft ground.

A second burst of gunfire tore out that clattered into the box to his side and the wagon above his back. He stopped trying to slip out and looked up, seeing a man hurrying closer with his gun thrust out.

The man was heading towards Dalton and so he presented a clear target. Dalton fired twice, his first shot being wild while the second shot clipped the running man's shoulder, making him drop.

Dalton kept low while he reloaded, which proved to be a difficult task when constrained and so he had to squirm forward before he could complete the action. Then he looked up to find the wounded man was on his knees and struggling to hold his gun steady.

The man saw that Dalton was ready to take him on and so he splayed lead at him. The shots were wild and clipped the box, and so Dalton took steady aim.

His shot sliced high into the man's chest making him keel over to the side. Then an ominous creak sounded.

The sustained gunfire had clipped the box and it was teetering and no longer looking as if it could support the wagon.

Dalton moved quickly, but he wasn't quick enough and the box tipped to the side making the wagon slam down on his legs. Dalton screeched in pain as both his good and his injured leg were driven into the ground.

The next few moments passed in a blur as he struggled to concentrate.

He gritted his teeth and willed himself to take account of what was happening. When he looked up, through pained eyes he saw Judah Sundown standing before him, considering his predicament with glee and an aimed gun.

CHAPTER 15

Dalton held his gun slackly and was lying awkwardly. It would take him several moments to raise the gun and aim, while Judah had already taken aim at him.

'I should have finished you off on the ridge,' Judah said.

'Except you didn't,' Dalton said. 'You were too busy ordering the death of a young girl.'

Judah raised a hand, ordering an unseen man who was standing beyond the wagon to stay back and, presumably, to keep Remington busy. Dalton thought back through the gunfight and he figured that only one of Judah's men was still alive.

'You don't know the full story of why I did that.'

'I'm sure you don't, or you wouldn't have wanted Sera dead.'

Judah shook his head. 'She was Edwidge Star's daughter, not mine; that's why he paid the blackmail money.'

'Marietta told Edwidge that Sera was his, but that was a lie.'

'What does that mean?' Judah muttered, his gun hand tightening as he narrowed his eyes.

Dalton sneered. 'It means you tried to kill your own daughter.'

Judah flinched back in surprise for a half pace, and his gun drifted away from Dalton for a mite.

'I'd never do that, but that doesn't matter as you're lying. Marietta never once spoke to me about Sera.'

Dalton looked Judah up and down, and then snorted with derision.

'Do you think she'd want anyone to know Sera's father is you?'

This comment hit home as Judah's eyes glazed and his gun arm twitched. So with him distracted, Dalton seized what might be his only chance. He twisted the gun in his grip and jerked up the weapon.

Judah saw what Dalton intended to do, but he was still slow to get his wits about him and fire, giving Dalton enough time to blast a shot low into his guts that made him fall forward.

As Judah's gun dropped to the ground, Dalton tried to raise himself to see the other gunman, and his movements became more frantic when gunfire tore out from beyond his vision.

Someone screeched and to his left a man stepped into view. Dalton turned his gun towards him, but with a relieved sigh he stilled his fire and nodded at Remington, who walked on to stand over Judah.

'Is that true?' Judah murmured, clutching his

blooded belly. 'Is Sera mine?'

Remington sighted Judah down the barrel of his gun.

'Nah,' he said.

He didn't fire when his taunt took the fight out of Judah and he slumped to lie face down in the mud. Judah didn't move again, but Remington still checked he was dead before he tasked himself with moving the wagon off Dalton's legs.

Remington couldn't help him alone, but with the gunmen dead, customers emerged from the saloon to help tip it over. While Dalton massaged his legs, Remington gathered up the box and set it on the back of the wagon.

Then he straightened the wheel and strained to get the wagon moving. Once it was rolling, to the townsfolk's bemusement, he shoved the wagon on to the corner.

When he'd manoeuvred it past the corner, the slope beyond the saloon took control of the wagon and, as Dalton had planned originally, it rolled from view. It headed down to the creek, the broken wheel making the wagon rattle and scrape along loudly and letting Dalton follow its unseen progress.

When the wagon tipped into the water, the watching townsfolk started murmuring uncertainly and Remington turned away to find Dalton was sitting on the edge of the boardwalk. Dalton flexed his bad leg gingerly and, when he decided it hadn't suffered any further damage, he smiled at Remington.

'I reckon we both did well there,' he said, 'but why did you push the wagon into the water?'

Remington returned the smile and held out a hand to help Dalton to his feet.

'As Marietta said,' he said, 'that money brings nothing but pain and death to whoever has it. So while we still had it, our problems would never end.'

'So you're really not concerned about the money?' Dalton asked when he'd eaten the dinner Marietta had provided.

'The money's gone,' Marietta said, not meeting his eye. 'Others might find it, and if they do I hope it brings them as much trouble as it brought me.'

Since Marietta had brought her daughter back to town, Sera had been more animated than Dalton had ever seen, and so Marietta had let her leave her room to sit with them while they ate.

Sera was resting quietly in a chair in the corner, but she had eaten the broth Marietta had fed her and she'd even taken the spoon herself for a few mouthfuls.

Dalton wished he could stay to watch her recovery, but he didn't feel he should as Marietta was still treating him coldly now he knew the secret about Sera's father.

'I hope,' Dalton said, 'not having the money brings you two, as well as Sera, happiness in the future.'

'And I hope,' Remington said, 'having your

reward brings you some joy.'

Dalton nodded, but mentioning the future made Marietta frown.

'I do too, and thank you,' she said in her usual matter of fact manner, 'but you'll be leaving now.'

This time Dalton accepted her order and stood up.

'I'll stay here tonight,' he said. 'In the morning, I'll leave.'

Then he headed to Sera's chair and knelt down on his good leg. She looked at him and smiled.

'Thank you for everything,' she said, her voice small, but strong. Even better, she was aware she'd spoken softly as she coughed and repeated her comment in a stronger voice.

'I did nothing,' Dalton said, remembering Remington's lament on Lonetree hill. 'I only helped Remington.'

From the corner of his eye, he saw Marietta nod and Remington smiled, but he met Sera's gaze while he had her concentration.

'You carried me from High Pass,' Sera breathed. 'You fought for me. You brought me back here. You saved my life.'

'You're mistaking me for Remington.' Dalton laid a hand on her arm. 'You've been hurt and you're still confused. Rest.'

Sera looked at him with doubt, but her longest conversation since her injury had tired her and she looked away. Her gaze sought out Remington before she closed her eyes and so with that, Dalton stood up and, without looking at the others, he headed to the door.

'Thank you,' Remington said.

Dalton turned and inclined his head, but he couldn't resist asking one final question.

'One matter still troubles me,' he said. 'I moved the box containing the money and which is now in the creek. It was surprisingly light and easy to manoeuvre, almost as if there was never anything in it in the first place.'

Marietta offered him a small smile, as did Remington.

'That matter,' she said, 'will have to continue troubling you.'